Romance
Under Wraps

by

Michele Jones

PrimaCasa Press, Lower Burrell, PA 15068

PrimaCasa Press is an Imprint of AIW Press, LLC.

https://aiwpress.com

ISBN-10: 1-9449-3812-5
ISBN-13: 978-1-944938-12-3

Dedication

To my husband, Brian, for his support, bending his ear, long sleepless nights, and missed meals. To my children, Krista and Zachary, for being there for me and listening to endless scenes and providing their feedback. And finally, a big shout out to my family and friends for supporting me.

Thank you all for believing in me and making my dream of being a writer come true.

At the ordained hour, they will rise
To try and prevent their demise
Once each century, time so short
Then present their findings to our court

The king to answer every question
Posed to him in precise succession
His advisor must provide him aid
Else both will fail when hearts are weighed

But one alternative is provided
Before their destinies are decided
Their once loved queen to seek and find
Win her favor, hearts entwined

Then with her live as blood and bone
The other with only his sins to atone

CHAPTER ONE

Even with no sundial to mark the passing of hours and days in the infernal darkness of his sarcophagus, Zet knew without question a century had passed. Every cell in his linen-wrapped body vibrated with the knowledge that he was about to rise again, if only for mere weeks, solstice to solstice.

He'd had no ability to move, to see, to feel for the last hundred years. All he'd done was lie there, listening to his own thoughts broken only by the trivial ramblings of the humans around him. Today, however, those banal conversations might prove useful. Today he would be free, and what those humans spoke of could be of some benefit to him. So instead of trying in vain to tune them out, he focused on them.

"Where are you, Mr. Shalhoub?" a woman asked. "Stuck on the bridge. … A wreck. … The weather. … I understand. … Everything's already here. …We've almost finished unloading. … When you get here come to the loading docks. Bay three. Ring the buzzer and security will let you in, they're expecting you."

"Hey, put that down," another woman said to the guard.

"Thanks for your help, guys. We'll take it from here," the first woman said. "You're free to go."

"Let's start uncrating. Hand me that crowbar."

"Wait a minute."

Zet lay still in the darkness. No matter how many times he did this over the centuries, he still hated being closed in, loathed the blackness, detested summoning the patience required not to reveal himself to the people outside his infernal sarcophagus.

He listened to shuffling and muttered voices, then nothing. Could he move? Curses, not yet. They hadn't freed him. A door slammed, followed by a dragging-screeching noise that pierced the quiet. At least his gods had given him the ability to speak and understand all languages, although he communicated to his advisor Dene only in his native tongue. What he wouldn't give to be free, to be whole, to have a look around. The hunger had returned. To have just a sip of a drink, just to clear the dust and be able to say anything to anyone.

"Here," a woman said. "Crowbar."

So they were still in the room.

He expected them to pry open his crate, for metal nails to squeak as they were pried out of wooden planks. But… nothing. She asked for a crowbar, then naught but quiet. No noise, no talking. Nothing. Dead silence.

He'd had enough of such stillness over his last waiting period. It was time for him to rise again. Their reticence was driving him crazy. Why wouldn't they just uncrate him?

"We should wait for Mr. Shalhoub." That same woman again. More silence. Not knowing drove him mad.

"C'mon, Tayla."

Ah, so the one in charge was named Tayla. The other was pushier. Hopefully Tayla gave in soon.

"No, we should wait," Tayla replied.

"He's stuck on the bridge. Who knows how long he'll be? We can take a quick peek and close it back up before he gets here."

"I don't know…"

"C'mon. This is the delivery we have been waiting our whole lives for. And this crate?"

Zet flinched when three sharp raps vibrated the box surrounding him.

"This one is labeled 'sarcophagus.'"

"Meredith, we really shouldn't." Another round of silence. Tayla needed to listen to her insistent friend, to give him what he desperately desired—a view of his surroundings.

Wait. Did the crate move? Thank the gods. How fortunate. Meredith convinced her to open the crate. Finally, to be able to look around.

"Okay," Tayla said, "but we've got to be careful. We don't want to damage the sarcophagus."

Something creaked. He heard grunting and hard breathing. A prying sound. Then nothing, total quiet. Did they give up?

A light thud. More prying, scraping, and grunting. Bangs and thuds. Did the girls finish removing the crate?

His body started tingling. He could wiggle his fingers and toes. The smell of the earthy, musty cloth invaded his nose. It would not be long now. It was almost time. He would be free of his prison, if only for a short time.

He could feel his muscles stretching, filling out. His nose itched and his body radiated heat. The time had arrived. No further need for the girls. He took shape in the shadows, behind several unopened crates. Soon he would be joined by his advisor, his confidant, his teacher — Dene. The gods had them connected.

Those girls. Something about those girls. He stared at them and focused on their conversation.

"This is much bigger than we thought," Tayla said, staring at the sarcophagus. "Let's go to the exhibit and check out the space. I think we need to make a change."

Zet looked them over. Something about the girl with the creamy skin and auburn hair called to him. He stared at her. As they turned from the sarcophagus and walked toward the door, he saw it. On her left shoulder. Could it be? Her symbol. The Goddess with two arrows crossed over a shield.

He sank back farther into the shadows, trying to wrap his head around what he'd just seen.

#

Would he ever be free of the curse? Damn it, Dene. Why couldn't one of us find her—preferably me. Get her to choose so the judgments could be over. No more sitting back, waiting. The time had come for him to take charge.

Light filtered into the room as the door opened. A man's voice controlled the conversation.

"Yeah, I just got here, traffic crawled on the bridge... The storm caused an accident... The team started without me. I won't work too late."

Where was Dene? Why had not he appeared yet? Zet watched as the man searched the wall for something. When he found it, it lit up the room. Amazing—the man held no candle, yet there was light. The man's face turned red as he crossed to the open crate, kicking the packaging that littered the floor.

"I've got to go… I love you, too… Good bye."

Zet watched the man check his sarcophagus. He ran his hands along its edges and across the top, pausing briefly at times then continuing. Zet had had enough lurking in the shadows. He took shape next to his sarcophagus and stretched his hands toward the man.

The man's mouth moved, but nothing came out. His body shook, and the color drained from his cheeks. He stumbled back, hands extended, protecting his face.

The mummy looked at the man and laughed.

The frightened man just gawked and backed away from him. "What's your name?"

The man just shook his head and backed further away.

Zet stalked him. "Name?"

"Sha… Shalhoub."

Zet smiled.

The door burst open and a guard came in, gun drawn.

Zet moved fast. He materialized behind the guard and snaked his arm across the front of his neck, settling the crook of his elbow under his chin. He grabbed his wrist with his other hand, driving his forearm into his neck and applying pressure.

The guard struggled to free himself, but the mummy applied more pressure, cutting off his airway. Within a minute, his body went limp and Zet dropped him. Shalhoub pointed at him. He opened his mouth to speak, but again, nothing came out.

Zed couldn't risk getting caught. He needed help. Someone to assist him. He turned to Shalhoub.

It would be so much easier if my fingers were not wrapped. Zet fumbled to pull the guard out of sight. For the love of Isis and Osiris, this was difficult. After several failed attempts, he succeeded. Thank the gods.

He needed to finish what he started. But not here, it would be messy, and he had no means to clean up. He grabbed the flint knife that had been buried with him for his protection. He hefted the guard across his shoulders, securing his legs with his arm. He turned to Shalhoub. "If you value your life, you will do as I say. You will help us dispose of the body. Make sure we will not get caught."

Shalhoub just stood there — stuttering, staring, shaking.

"Help me get him out of here."

Zet planned to dump the body in the river once he got outside. He hauled him through the door and looked around. Concrete and tall buildings. No river, no bridge. Only land and concrete. And rain. Not just rain, but a fierce storm.

How he hated rain, especially heavy rain. It limited him. It forced him to remain inside in his mummy state. He couldn't risk ruining his wrappings. He needed more time to completely transform to his human state.

Zet searched the area. He needed to get rid of the body. A few feet ahead and to his left he spied large metal trash bins under an overhang. Not his first choice, but it would have to do. He used his knife to finish the job. Shalhoub flinched, blanched, and looked as though he were about to wretch.

"Shalhoub, toughen up and toss the body into that rubbish receptacle."

"The dumpster?"

"Dumpster? Ha. I like that. Yes. Dispose of him in the dumpster, then come with me inside. We have much to do, and little time in which to do it."

Zet gestured toward the guard with the knife, and Shalhoub managed to throw the body into the dumpster. Once the guard was disposed of, they went back inside. Zet wasn't kidding. He had plans, and he needed Shalhoub.

Zet communicated to Dene. *The gods are working in our favor. I have the perfect plan for us. We must speak.*

CHAPTER TWO

Tayla didn't believe in the pharaoh's curse. She had been perfectly comfortable while working on the exhibit, but sitting in the break room having a coffee, a flash of light outside the window startled her.

"It's just a storm. It's just a storm. This damn debacle with the Egyptian Exhibit. I shouldn't have even been here tonight."

A shiver tingled her spine. How could she work in a museum and not be afraid of the five-thousand-year-old mummy in a sarcophagus, but a storm made her anxious?

Outside the lightning lit up the sky and thunder boomed fiercely, rattling the windows.

"That's it. I need to have some M&Ms." She walked over to the vending machine and fed in a few dollars, getting three bags of

M&Ms. When she sat down, she opened a napkin, poured out all three bags, and started sorting them by color.

A shuffling sound came from the hall. Tayla jumped, causing her chair to slide back and hit into the table behind her. The lightning flashed more frequently, and thunder boomed even louder. Tayla sorted the M&Ms even faster—brown, red, yellow, orange, blue, green.

The storm put on a show, and the last lightning flash shot sparks into the sky. It looked like the fireworks from the Fourth, then the lights flickered and the power went out.

"Great. Just great."

Tayla had just finished sorting her M&Ms and knew where each color had been moved to on the napkin. Her hands trembled. Time to eat her candy, brown first.

The only light in the room came from the dimly lit red T in the exit sign and the sporadic lightning flashes. Tayla cringed. Thunderstorms, she hated them. Rain was okay, but not the fireworks and sonic booms taking place outside. When the lightning strike lit up the room she saw a man standing in front of her, and the T in the exit sign faded and started blinking.

"Stan, is that you?"

No answer.

Tayla felt the sweat trickle down her forehead, and her hands started shaking. The only way out of the break room had been blocked by the mystery man. Maybe she imagined him. After all, thunderstorm storms really freaked her out.

Her eyes had still hadn't adjusted to the lack of light, but the storm outside kept lighting up the room, and it was empty. The T in the exit sign lit brightly and then fizzled out completely. Now her only light source came from outside. She took a few calming breaths and kept eating the M&Ms—she finished the brown and red and had started eating the yellow ones. The storm picked up in intensity. Lightning lit up the empty room several times. It must have been her imagination. She continued popping M&Ms into her mouth as she looked for her flashlight.

The storm raged on, but despite her fears, she kept telling herself there was nothing and nobody to be afraid of. Then she heard it again—a shuffling sound. Why didn't she just go home? She could have finished what she was working on Monday morning. But no, she had to get it done. She twisted her long black hair into a bun at the base of her neck, securing it with the hair tie she always kept on her wrist. She knew from her self-defense training that her hair could be used against her. This ensured that it wouldn't.

Next, she pulled the flashlight from her purse as she shoved more M&Ms into her mouth. Lightning flashed and lit up the room. Tayla saw a man holding something in his hand standing just a few feet in front of her table.

"Who's there?" she asked.

Really? Who's there? Wow. Was she really expecting an answer? And seriously, what would it be? 'It's me, the killer?' She'd seen enough scary movies to know—it was always the stupid girl who gets it. She needed to stop being so stupid.

She dropped the flashlight when she pushed away from the table and looked for something to defend herself. She should have just finished what she was working on and left. If she didn't need the coffee, she would be done, or at least in her office where she had several things to use in self-defense.

She grabbed a chair, her best option, and wondered if the aluminum frame would be enough to hurt the man with the knife and allow her to get away. She raised the chair to swing it, and lightning flashed. An empty room filled her vision, no man, no knife. She spun quickly as the lightning flashed, but saw no one.

Tayla dropped the chair. It banged off the table and bounced before landing on its side. She plopped down in her chair and felt around for the flashlight. Switching it on, she shined it around the break room. Empty. Where did he go?

She shook her head. "It must be my imagination."

The shuffling noise got louder. A lump rose in her throat, her heart beat faster, and her hands shook as she tried to pick up the M&Ms. That wasn't her imagination. Again, she shined the flashlight around the empty room. She spun in all directions, and as she spun, her flashlight dimmed, and then died.

The room was almost pitch black. Without her flashlight or the lightning flashes, she couldn't see more than a foot in front of her. She needed to get out of there, immediately. Think, Tayla, Think. Her phone. It had a full battery and a flashlight app. Another lightning flash, and again she saw someone standing in front of her. She lifted another chair and was about to swing it when the lights came on.

Meredith stood before her, hands raised to protect herself. To her right sat a cart containing plaques for the exhibit.

"Tayla, what are you doing? For God's sake, put the chair down before you hurt someone."

Tayla's breath came fast and hard. Her hands trembled as she struggled to put the chair down before she slumped against the table. Her palms ached from the nail marks embedded in them, sustained while gripping the chair.

"Didn't you see him?" Tayla asked.

"See who?" Meredith replied. "We're the only two people here. Well, except for Security in the exhibits."

Tayla followed Meredith's eyes as she looked down at the table.

"Seriously, Tayla, you're on the green ones? It's just a little storm. There's nothing to worry about."

"There was a man. With a knife. I saw him. He stood right where you're standing now. I heard him. He made a shuffling noise."

"There is no man, and the noise that you heard had to be me pushing that old cart. Now, let's get out of here."

Meredith put her arm around Tayla's shoulder and grabbed the cart with her free hand. The cart whined as she pulled.

Tayla heard it—that shuffling sound. It was Meredith, she didn't lift her feet while dragging the cart.

"I know I saw something. Are you sure you didn't pass anyone?"

"Honestly, Tayla, I didn't pass anyone. Let's get this stuff put away and go home. There's nothing here we can't do next week."

#

Tayla glanced at the two pewter frames that stood on either side of the clock on her mantle—her family and her boyfriend. She missed them both. Her parents were visiting her sister in Texas and her boyfriend, Bennett, had been working long hours, and they hadn't spent much time together. Even when she stopped by to see him, he had to hurry off to the next patient.

Tayla hummed along with her iPod as she straightened up the living room. Date night, and their five-year anniversary. No work, no phone—just the two of them enjoying each other's company. Dinner at a local restaurant then catching the latest movie. Hopefully a walk through the park before coming back to her place for dessert, wine, and romance. Bennett told her to keep tonight open.

After a quick shower, Tayla rummaged through her closet for the perfect outfit. Something that showed Bennett what he'd been missing, but wasn't over the top. He'd cancelled date night every week for the past two months for work and a family emergency. So she'd kept busy—visiting with her parents, going out with Meredith, but her heart longed for Bennett.

Pleated pants, a cami, and a sheer lace over shirt. She stepped in front of the mirror to finish her hair and makeup, then she'd be ready.

Her heart fluttered. She loved date night, especially tonight, their anniversary. Bennett's job, his family, and his aggressive study schedule took up most of his free time. That made date night so special. Time all to themselves.

Her phone buzzed—Grand Concourse.

She smiled. Just thinking about how Bennett got her phone number brought back a sweet memory.

Tayla had sat in the emergency room with a t-shirt wrapped around her arm. Blood seeped through her makeshift bandage. Hopefully they would see her soon. She had argued with Meredith about coming. Thankfully her friend insisted, because her arm hadn't stopped bleeding and the muscles throbbed.

She couldn't believe she still sat waiting. Almost two hours had passed, and only two people had been taken back. The t-shirt she had around the wound needed replacing because it had soaked through, and blood had started dripping onto the floor.

She watched as Meredith had a heated conversation with the admitting clerk and came away with a towel for her to wrap around her arm.

The room spun and her stomach churned. She didn't remember passing out. But there she was, lying on a bed, arm wrapped in gauze, Meredith at her left side, nurse at the right.

The curtain parted, and the most handsome young doctor walked in and smiled at her. "I'm Doctor Bennett Cartwright." He tried to dismiss Meredith, but Tayla refused to let her leave. He conceded and asked the usual patient questions before asking what happened. Both she and Meredith said, "Work accident," at the same time, and let out a small laugh.

As he peeled the bandage from the wound, Tayla jerked. His touch sent chills up her arm. He'd said she'd been numbed, and she knew she shouldn't feel anything in her arm, but she did. Her entire body hummed. The conversation turned casual as he stitched her up.

"Dr. Cartwright—"

"Please, call me Bennett."

She tried blowing a stray hair away from her face, unsuccessfully.

He reached up and pushed it away from her face, and his hand brushed her cheek. She sucked in a deep breath and held it. Her face must have been on fire.

"A nurse will be back shortly to take you out." He wrote up her discharge papers, and instructed Meredith to get the car.

"But, I can—"

"Hospital policy. You do want to go home, don't you?"

"Okay, I'll take the free ride."

She smiled, and he smiled back as he parted the curtains and left the room.

The nurse handed her the papers and went over his directions, only pausing when she realized he didn't leave the prescription.

"I'll be right back," the nurse said and ducked out.

Moments later Dr. Cartwright came back, alone.

"I'm sorry. Here you go."

As she reached to take it from him, he pulled it back.

"I'll give this to you on one condition."

"What's that?"

"You give me your phone number."

She smiled at the memory and refocused on the phone. Tayla texted back, *See you soon. Just walk in.*

Wow. Grand Concourse. Tayla needed to change. She swapped her casual clothes for a little black dress. She needed something else. She put on a pearl choker, her grandmother's ring, and his favorite perfume—an earthy, mossy, sweet scent with a hint with of vanilla, and one he had created just for her by Clive Christian. A dab on the wrist, another behind the ears, and one more on the neck. Subtle but noticeable. Stilettos and a small black beaded purse completed her outfit.

A hint of a smile crossed her lips and she danced across the floor. He wanted to make their five-year anniversary special. Her gift to him would have to be opened here. A key to the house and tickets to the theater.

#

She heard his car and went to the mirror for one last check of her hair and makeup. He walked through the door moments later, crossed the room, grabbed her around the waist, and pulled her in for a long kiss.

He broke the kiss, and she came up breathing fast and heavy.

"You look amazing."

"So do you," she replied.

He inhaled deeply. "And you wore my favorite perfume. Have I told you how much I love you?" He smiled and his brown eyes twinkled.

"I love you, too." She leaned in and kissed his neck.

He tilted her head up and bent down, crushed his lips onto hers, and kissed her deeply while gently rubbing her back. He broke the kiss and pulled her even closer to him. "We have to leave, or we'll lose our reservation."

"We could stay here," she managed to get out.

He looked at her with those sable eyes and smiled. "Later."

"Wait, before we go, I have something for you." She pulled out the envelope containing theater tickets. "Go on, open it."

Bennett strode to her desk and grabbed her letter opener. He slid it inside the envelope, meticulously sliding it from left to right. Once open, he reached in and pulled out the tickets. He stared at them for a minute before responding, "Lion King. I love it." He leaned in and kissed her, then tucked the tickets inside his jacket pocket.

"I have something else for you when we get back from dinner."

He licked his lips. "If it's what I think it is, I can hardly wait."

#

They walked into the restaurant, his arm behind her back. He kissed her cheek and let go, stepping to the podium to confirm their reservation. Tayla watched as he slipped the man some money. Seconds later they were escorted to a cozy booth, away from the rest of the patrons.

Bennett declined the menus and asked for their waiter. The man nodded and their server appeared shortly. He ordered a bottle of Dom Perignon. Before the server left to bring the champagne, Bennett whispered something to him.

Tayla's body tingled. Before she could speak, their server returned and served the champagne.

"A toast to the most beautiful woman, both inside and out." He smiled as he lifted his glass.

Tayla felt her face get warm. "I can't believe you did this. Thank you. I've missed our date nights."

He reached across the table and took her hand in his. "I love you."

"I love you, too."

They made small talk and sipped on the champagne. He gently pulled his free hand from hers and reached into his pocket. Then he placed a little black box in front of her.

Tayla's heart beat faster. Could it be? Her hands trembled.

He opened the box, and an emerald ring reflected in the light. She slumped slightly in her booth.

"I saw this and thought of you. Do you like it?"

"It's beautiful," she whispered.

"What's wrong?"

He reached across the table and touched her cheek. "If you don't like it, we can take it back."

"No. I love it. Thank you."

"It matches your eyes. But the ring pales in comparison to you."

Her face felt warm. She had to be blushing. "We should eat."

Bennett motioned for the server, and asked for menus He poured them each another glass of champagne and that emptied the second the bottle. Their conversation turned to something lighter and he reached for her hand. The server returned with a third bottle and took their order.

As the server walked away, Bennett pulled his cell out of his jacket pocket and placed it on the table.

Tayla's nostrils flared, and her eyes narrowed. "You're breaking your rule. No phones on date night."

He pulled his hand from hers. "Tayla, please. Don't be like that."

"Put it away."

"You're being ridiculous."

"I'm not. It's our anniversary. Let's have just one night without you looking at the phone."

"It's my job. I need to be accessible."

"Can't we get through dinner without it?"

His phone rang.

"Don't answer that."

He looked at the screen. "I have to take this."

He excused himself and took the call. Minutes later he returned. "I'm sorry, but I have to go." He remained standing and motioned for the server.

"Are you serious?" Tears formed in the corner of her eyes.

"I can't believe you're acting like this. I'm doing this for us."

"Really? For us? Tonight is supposed to be about us. You scheduled tonight off months ago. It's our anniversary. Just us. No work. No email. No phones. The others don't work on their days off. How many time have you filled in for them? We haven't had time to ourselves for months, and you're cancelling our date night again. We need to have some us-time."

"You're being selfish."

"I'm not being selfish. I just wanted to spend time with my boyfriend."

"Don't make a scene."

"Fine. Just take me home."

"I don't have time. I've called you a cab." He leaned in, kissed her on the forehead, turned, and headed for the door, leaving her sitting at the table, alone.

Tayla stared as he walked out. The little black box sat open on the table, the ring gleaming in the light. She picked up the box and closed it. She wanted to throw it across the room. Instead she dropped it in her purse and stood up to leave.

As she headed toward the door, their server flagged her down.

"Shall I have the chef prepare your dinners to go?"

"Oh. Uh. Yes, please."

"Shall I put this on your credit card, or do you prefer to pay cash?"

Tayla handed him her card.

"I'll be right back with your dinners, and you receipt."

The nerve of him. He had the manners to call her a cab, but he stuck her with the bill. Fabulous. And she thought they were getting engaged.

Tonight sucked.

CHAPTER THREE

Dene found himself in a basement holding room. He began searching around and determined they had been sent to another museum. Where had they been sent to this time? He slipped into the hall. Only dim light illuminated the walls. He needed to know where they had been sent.

He made his way to a desk with mechanical equipment marked, "Egypt, Ancient and Modern." Dene touched the button and the machine came to life. It showed the pyramids, the Nile, and present day Egypt. Every minute or so, he looked around. He didn't want to get caught.

He noticed several things missing from ancient Egyptian life. How can they know both so much and so little? He shook his head. After turning off the machine, he moved on, searching for clues to his location. There were several signs. He knew where they had been sent, and he needed to get to his king. Dene started walking cautiously toward the exit. After only a few steps, the museum lost all power. All praise to you Isis. Thank you for your assistance. This would enable him to get to Zet without setting off an alarm.

#

"Pennsylvania. The Egyptian government sent us to Pennsylvania. Tell me, how am I supposed to find my queen, my true love, when I'm not even in Egypt?"

"Your true love?"

Dene glared at him.

The king sighed and fluffed him off with a wave of his hand. "We must keep searching. This time, we will find her."

Dene's face drooped, his eyes lowered, and his body sagged. Endless searching and several millennia had passed. Yet they hadn't had any luck. Egypt was where they needed to be.

"I'm certain she isn't here. We are at the Carnegie Museum of Natural History in Pittsburgh. This search is futile." He tried to convince his king. "We need to get back to Egypt to be successful."

The king's nostrils flared and his face turned red. "The gods sent us here. We will continue our search. My destiny depends upon your success."

Dene's hands trembled. "It's your fault we're in this situation to begin with. If you had been a kind and fair ruler, we would both have entered the afterlife. Our gods spared you because of your queen and my mother. They are the reason you have this second chance."

The king raised his wrapped hand. "You will not speak to me in such a tone." He flicked his wrist and sent Dene back into a suspended state.

Dene knew he needed to find his queen. Zet would never learn. He failed several of the gods' tests—and the weighing of the heart ceremony. Too much time had passed. He hated being caught in this suspended state. He wanted to cross over. He had to try, so he called upon the gods for help.

Isis, Anubis, and Osiris appeared before him.

"Not all is as it seems," they said in unison.

"Search and you shall find her," Isis whispered.

They vanished before he could ask any questions.

Another long night. He wished he could forget, as the queen had, but that was part of the curse. His king ruined several lives. Now they both had to atone for his mistakes. Well, Dene had made one mistake of his own for which he had to atone.

Isis's words echoed in his head. *Seek and you shall find her.* Could she really be found here, in this foreign land? If he found her, would she recognize him? What if she were taken? Could finding her really free him and give his king a second chance? Would his king repent?

Dene sighed and closed his eyes. Her face flashed in his mind—alabaster skin, kohl-lined blue eyes, amber hair, and a smile that could part the Nile.

He hated that his existence depended on an evil king who ruined lives, who needed to repent. And couldn't the gods tell him where to find his queen instead of being so cryptic?

Finally, his king summoned him to continue his search. Dene appeared in the basement holding room before Zet. He grabbed his coin and rubbed it, flipping it between his fingers.

"You must continue my lessons and the search for my queen, for my sake. Your constant lamentation is hindering you, keeping you from freeing me. But I have taken action, and I have a plan."

He brought forth the Shalhoub. "This is Siamun Shalhoub, the collections manager for my exhibit."

Dene felt his stomach lurch. What had Zet done?

"Shalhoub will be helping us. We will be staying with him. He will even let us work on the exhibit, giving us access here. Ability to come and go freely, without these pesky Carnegies to question us."

"They are Pennsylvanians," Shalhoub said. "From Pittsburgh. They only work here at the Carnegie Museum."

"Immaterial." Zet waved his linen-clad hand and spoke to Dene. "This access will give you time to search for the queen and teach me my next lesson."

Dene's stomach roiled. "Why is he helping us?"

Shalhoub answered. "I have no choice—that is, if I want to live."

Dene stared at Zet. " You've ruined my life thousands of times over. Not only must I search for our queen and teach you what you need to gain entrance to the afterlife, now I must add labors at this institution and protections of this collections manager to my list of duties for you. You are mad."

"It is your destiny to serve me. The queen is here. I have seen her. And I have a plan for you to get her. You shall meet her tomorrow. I was drawn to her, and you will be too. I will—I mean, one of us will gain her favor, and then your tedious lessons will be rendered moot, anyway. This time, we will be free."

#

Dene paced Siamun Shalhoub's accommodations. He hated everything Zet had done. Everything he would continue to do. Zet did nothing if it did not benefit him.

"What would you have me do? How may I be of service to you?" Dene asked Zet, though he knew what the answers would be.

You should be more appreciative. I obtained what we need to succeed in this century. Follow my instructions and the curse shall be broken.

If Zet were right, could this girl he found really be the one? Dene doubted it.

Dene rubbed the coin in his pocket. Things in this century had changed greatly since he was last alive. The gods gave them some help acclimating, but there was much to learn.

Shalhoub had agreed to assist Zet. Well, he had no choice. He would not be a trusted ally. For now, he shared his clothes, his accommodations, his transportation. Transportation did not matter. He could get where he needed to go. Both of them were at Zet's mercy.

Dene paced the house they shared, hoping this time Zet could be taught and pass the weighing of the heart ceremony. He had little faith that they would find the queen. Time ticked by, and his search would start tomorrow. The gods always provided what they needed. This time would be no different. He reached in his pocket and pulled out a wallet. Inside, a little plastic card.

"Shalhoub, what is this 'Platinum American Express' flat? Do I take it to a money exchanger in trade for gold?"

Shalhoub shook his head and sighed. "In a sense. You use it in place of gold or money. When you go to a store, make your selections, then present it to the clerk. They take it in place of money."

"So I can only use it once. What then if I wish to make additional purchases elsewhere?"

"No. They don't keep it. They scan it and give it back to you. Like a debit in a ledger."

"Fascinating." Plastic money, easier to carry than gold. Another useful invention.

After settling into his room he went through the clothes Shalhoub gave him. Nothing fit. The clothes hung loosely on him and were not to his liking. Three suits and several white dress shirts, nothing for daily wear. Dene groaned. Definitely nothing he would wear. In the bottom of the bag was a colored picture of Shalhoub's family that read, "Come Home Soon Papa. Love Kali." His stomach churned and his body sagged. Again he shoved his hand in his pocket and rubbed his coin. He would not let Zet ruin this man's life.

How many lives would Zet destroy so that he could be happy — free from a curse of his own making.

Tomorrow would be a long day, and he had much to do. He lay across the bed and closed his eyes, but he couldn't stop thinking. Had Zet found the queen? What about the man whose life had been cut short so that Zet could be happy? Shalhoub told him what had happened. Dene could not be sure if Shalhoub trusted him, hated him, or feared him. He tossed and turned before falling into a restless slumber.

#

Monday arrived quicker than he wanted. He definitely needed another day to get himself ready. He would know the exhibit better than anyone, that wouldn't be an issue. But could Shalhoub really get him in as part of the team? Would he have the necessary documentation? Would they ask him any questions, and if so, would he know the answers? He reached into his pocket for his coin, rubbing it between his fingers.

Dene walked outside and stared out into the city. No sand, no grass, no trees — just concrete. Buildings taller than the pyramids, stacked too close to each other. Streets filled with cars going nowhere. The people flowed like the Nile, continually moving, swirling around obstacles in their path. He wrinkled his nose at the smell of coffee mixed with gas, cigarettes and cigars, combined with bread, sulfur, and cinnamon. He missed the smell of home, and the peace of his simpler life.

He left early, allowing himself time to walk. Dene clutched the coin in his pocket. He hated the big cities. After a deep breath, he merged into the pedestrian flow and made his way to the museum.

Shalhoub gave him paperwork with specific instructions regarding his assignment at the museum. He needed to get registered with security first, then he would be able to come and go at will, using the employee entrance and going through security. He shook his head. Had people really become so evil that they needed these precautions?

Dene entered the museum and followed the directions that had been printed, making his way to the security office. Once registered, he was escorted by a guard to the exhibit room.

He arrived early. Thank Isis, the room was empty.

Zet communicated to him. *I will be along as soon as Shalhoub gets my paperwork done. Make sure they feature me in a prominent spot. I must be the center of attention. And you must do something about the color in here. I hate it.*

Today is my first work day. Give me time to speak with the others. I haven't ev —

"I'm sorry, are you speaking to me?" a voice behind him said. "I'm afraid that my Egyptian Arabic is a bit rusty."

"Forgive me, I didn't realize I had been talking aloud. I am noticing the work that needs to be completed for the exhibit."

Two women crossed the room, and extended their hands. "I'm Tayla Amari, and this is Meredith Nazari. We'll be working with you on the exhibit."

Dene's body tingled, and his heart beat a bit faster. He felt connected, drawn to the women. Something he hadn't felt in a long time.

"Forgive my manners." He extended his hand. "I am Dene Tahan."

"Pleased to meet you," Tayla said.

Only here for a minute and already he felt apprehensive. He flipped the coin in his pocket.

Meredith went to the computer and printed him a name badge. "Wear this for now. I'll have security get you a new name badge."

"Thank you, Meredith. But my name is spelled D-E-N-E, not D-E-N-N-Y."

Meredith's face turned red. He wanted to comfort her. Could Zet be correct? Could his true love be found here, away from his homeland?

"Oh, I'm sorry, I—"

"You have not to be sorry. I understand your confusion." He needed to change the subject. "Shall we get started? We have much to do."

"We've printed all Mr. Shalhoub's emails," Tayla said. "Let's sit down and get started."

He had no idea what the emails said. Another issue that needed to be dealt with. He hesitated, unsure how to proceed.

"Dene? Is everything okay?" Meredith asked.

He turned and looked at her. Immediately, her eyes caught his attention. Cobalt, the same color as his queen. They sparkled as she spoke, and his body hummed.

He went to the table and took a seat. Everyone reached for the paper pile at the same time. His reflexes had been faster than either girl's, but Meredith, being closer, had brushed his hand.

Her touch made his arm tingle, and his heart beat a little faster.

"I do not have a copy of my email with me. Would you mind if I kept these?"

"Not at all. I'll print another copy and we can get started," Tayla said.

"Let's start with the sarcophagus placement. We'll place it in the center of the room and work the exhibit around it."

"But your email said you wanted the sarcophagus in the front of the room, on a raised platform," Tayla said.

Another mistake. A bead of perspiration formed on his upper lip.

"After looking at the exhibit hall, I believe it is best to showcase the sarcophagus in the center of the room. It would be best if we forget about the emails and start from scratch. When Shalhoub gets here, we should discuss thoughts about the exhibit arrangement."

He stood, walked to the trash can by the door, and threw the papers into it. Hopefully this would start them all off working together.

Michele Jones

CHAPTER FOUR

Tayla stared at her phone. Five days. He hadn't called or texted her in five days. At least Meredith was having better luck. She walked out with Zet after work last night.

She gathered her notes, fixed a travel mug of coffee, grabbed her coat, and headed out. No need to sit there and stew about what happened. She needed to take her mind off their failed anniversary date. At least she had the exhibit.

Even at this early hour, the parking lot was full. Damn it. There was a game that day. She'd have to park at Schenley and walk. She grabbed her tennis shoes from her gym bag and slipped them on.

"Good morning, Tayla, you're here early," the security guard said, motioning her inside.

"Hi, John. I've got a lot to do on the exhibit." She placed her bag on the belt and walked through the scanner. "Did I pass?"

The security guard chuckled. "Of course. Criminals don't go through security."

"Have a great day, John. Don't work too hard." She headed for the stairs.

Tayla slumped into her chair and pushed back from her desk. She picked her phone up again, hoping Bennett sent her a text, an email. Maybe she missed a call... But nothing. Was she being unreasonable? Did she make too much of him being on call during their date? She reached into her purse and pulled out the little black box.

She stared at the unopened box and ran her hand over it. Images of Bennett giving her the ring clouded her mind. Tired of dwelling on that failed date, she grabbed the box and shoved it back in her purse.

Not getting anything done sitting in her office, she grabbed her supplies, shoved them in her bag, and headed to the exhibit room. She heard noises in the hall leading to the room, but didn't see anyone. Lack of sleep and her fight with Bennett must be messing with her mind. John told her she had been the first to come in today, and only a few minutes had passed since she came in. It couldn't be Meredith, she never came in before nine. Those noises must be in her imagination.

Only emergency lighting lit the hall. Security would turn the lights on around eight. She heard the noise again, and someone yelling, but he wasn't yelling in English. It wasn't her imagination this time. It sounded like—no, it couldn't be, could it? Egyptian Arabic? She'd heard the language before, but nobody who worked here spoke it. And it sounded like whoever was speaking was quite angry.

She called security and crept toward the exhibit. As she got closer, the yelling got louder. A few feet ahead she could see the door to the exhibit slightly open, and light coming from inside. Tayla knew she locked before she left last night.

Tayla ducked around the corner and kept peeking at the door. Damn it. Where was security? She paced faster while she waited for them to get there. They could be destroying the exhibit or stealing from the museum.

The yelling grew more intense, and she heard several thuds.

What was taking security so long? Those thieves were ruining the exhibit. She heard footsteps coming closer and breathed a sigh of relief. Finally.

Three security guards headed her way, John leading them.

"You need to get out of here," John ordered. "Now."

"No way. I'm staying. I've got to check the exhibit. I need to make sure they don't leave with anything."

The shaking of his head and the scowl on his face let Tayla know he didn't approve. Tayla watched the group get closer to the exhibit, then they flung the door open and ran in with guns drawn. Minutes later they came out, guns holstered, no prisoners.

Tayla headed toward the room, but John stopped her.

"The room's empty," John said.

"That's — it can't — not possible. I heard yelling coming from the room, and loud banging noises. Maybe — "

"There's no one in there. The exhibit looks fine," John said.

"I know I heard someone arguing in there. Are you sure? Did you check everywhere?"

"The room is empty. No one is hiding in there, and there's no way out except for the door."

She just stared at him. She couldn't have imagined that.

"Thanks for checking it out. Maybe the noise came from outside."

Tayla ran into the room once she had been given the all clear. At first glance, everything looked just fine. But once she started looking more closely, it hit her. Nothing had been ruined, but the entire room had been rearranged. The statue place holders, the taped off sarcophagus, the interactive area, even the paint samples, all different.

Someone definitely had been in the room after they left yesterday. Tayla called John and asked him if anyone working on the exhibit came back to work after they left yesterday. She knew what his answer would be, and he confirmed it. No one had been there after they left. "I need to check the security footage. Someone was in that room."

"I already have. Sorry, Tayla. No one went into the exhibit room."

"But—the door was open. I heard yelling and noises."

"The door mustn't have latched. No one but the guards went near the exhibit."

Tayla grabbed her bag and left for the break room. Something just didn't add up.

#

Tayla made a cup of coffee, grabbed a couple bags of M&Ms, and headed to her office. Someone had been in that room and rearranged it. Security couldn't find any evidence, but things just didn't move on their own. Someone had to move them.

Punctual as usual, Meredith came in at exactly nine o'clock, followed by Dene and Shalhoub. She noticed that Zet held the door open for them. Meredith looked happy. Tayla shoved another handful of blue M&Ms into her mouth.

Meredith crossed the room and stood in front of her. "What's wrong?"

"Someone broke into the exhibit. I don't think anything is missing, but whoever broke in rearranged the entire room, and they even changed the paint colors. I got in early and went to do some blocking in the exhibit hall, as I got closer I heard something. Arguing, and not in English. It sounded like ancient Arabic, but I couldn't be sure. Then I heard thuds and scraping sounds. I called security. They checked it out but didn't find anything. And the security tapes were blank."

Tayla shoved another handful of blue M&Ms into her mouth. Her entire body shook with anger. "I waited for you so we could check out the exhibit more thoroughly."

"Are you sure? How would they get in? I have to go through security each time before I can get into the building," Dene said.

"What are we standing here for? Let's go," Meredith said.

Tayla threw her bag over her shoulder and headed for the door being held open by Dene this time. Meredith was already half way down the hall with Zet beside her, Shalhoub a few steps behind them, and she and Dene hurried to catch up. Within minutes, they were at the locked door to the exhibit. Meredith swiped her pass card and went in first, followed by the rest of them. After a brief scan of the room, she turned to Tayla.

"This is exactly how we left it yesterday."

Tayla stammered. "I—I—I don't understand. Only an hour ago everything was moved. Even the taped-off place for the sarcophagus."

Dene turned and faced Tayla. "Maybe you pictured a different layout in your head, and that is what you saw. You did say yesterday that you thought we should change the layout."

She shook her head. "I didn't imagine it."

"You have been working late. Maybe your imagination is playing tricks on you. This room looks exactly how we left it last night. The last five days we were here sixteen hours. I believe if you get some sleep, everything will be better."

"No." She looked around the room eyes wide. "Sleep isn't the problem. I couldn't have imagined it."

Meredith pulled her aside. "I made lunch plans for us today. It's been too long since we did anything. Maybe you're letting your fight with Bennett cloud your judgment."

"I don't want to talk about that."

"You need to talk about that. To resolve it. It's messing with your work."

"It's not."

"It is." Meredith put her arm around Tayla's shoulders. "We're doing lunch today, my treat. We're going to one of your favorites. What about Hello Bistro? I refuse to take no for an answer. Just you, me, and a great burger. I've been a terrible friend. I know you needed to talk, and I haven't been there."

Tayla smiled. She knew Meredith was right. This fight with Bennett had her all messed up. She couldn't truly focus on anything.

"I could really go for a good burger. I'm in."

Dene cleared his throat. "Let's get started. There is still much that needs to be done." Both Tayla and Meredith nodded and grabbed their bags. Tayla sat close to the easel and pulled out her markers. Meredith walked to the chair beside Tayla. Dene, Zet, and Shalhoub sat at the table around Shalhoub's iPad. Shalhoub tapped his fingers on the table. Maybe he saw something not right with the exhibit, too. She would ask him later.

She also thought something was going on with Zet and Meredith.

Meredith reached for a pile of papers at the same time as Zet, and he brushed her hand. Her cheeks turned a bright shade of red. Could things really be heating up between them? Why did that make her uncomfortable?

It's been two years since Meredith's messy breakup with Ethan. She hadn't wanted to see anyone, not even in a causal relationship. But why did she choose Zet?

The next four hours flew by, and they made great progress. Three different parts to the exhibit had been hashed out. The one that Tayla liked best—the interactive one. She loved the fact that children could play and learn.

However, the five of them couldn't decide on a paint color. As Tayla argued for a pale blue, her stomach growled. She blushed and looked at her watch. "I think we should break for lunch. It's one o'clock." She pushed back from the table, stood and stretched.

Zet stood and pulled Meredith's chair out for her.

Again, Tayla couldn't explain it, but she felt uneasy. Why did Zet showing Meredith affection bother her so much? She couldn't place it, but something just didn't sit right with her about Zet. Seeing him touch her and show her affection made her suspicious.

Zet flashed a dazzling smile at Meredith, then crossed the room to open the door for the group. "You're welcome to join me for lunch. I'm grabbing something from the cafeteria and taking it to the park."

"Thanks for the offer, but Tayla and I have plans. Maybe tomorrow?"

"They can all come—" She stopped when she saw the look on Meredith's face.

"You understand, don't you?" Meredith asked.

"Of course. See you both after lunch."

#

The restaurant was crowded. "Maybe we should just go back to the cafeteria. I have stuff in the fridge."

"No way. I said I was taking you out to lunch so that we could talk, and I meant it. Besides you need to talk and you won't at work. I know you."

Tayla sighed. "You're right. I am craving a good burger. And they make the best."

"It will be just a few minutes." The hostess took their names.

The girls watched as several groups of people left. Minutes later, they were seated as promised.

Tayla loved this place. Good food, fast friendly service, and close to the office. Tayla stared at the menu, but she knew exactly what she would get. A thick, juicy, rare burger with sautéed onions and bacon, a side salad, and an order of fries. Her go-to meal.

After placing their order, the waitress returned with their drinks and salads. Five minutes later, she came back with refills. Clearly Meredith planned on a long conversation.

"So," Meredith began.

"What's going on with you and Zet?" Tayla asked.

"Stop trying to change the subject. What's going on with you and Bennett? You've been moping around since your fifth anniversary date. I got your text about the Grand Concourse. I could tell you were excited. But then nothing. Spill it."

"We had a fight."

"I know that, you told me. Fess up. What really happened? You thought he was going to propose, and he didn't. Is that it?"

She sighed. "You know his rule about cell phones on date night, right? Well, he broke it. He took out his phone and took a call."

"That's it? That's what you're fighting about?"

"That's part of it." Tayla pulled the little black box out of her purse.

Meredith's eyes grew wide. "He proposed? He gave you a ring and you're not wearing it? Why didn't you tell me? What's wrong with you? I thought we were friends."

"Open the box."

She watched Meredith open the box and slump into her seat.

"So you're mad at him because he didn't propose?"

Tayla sighed. "No. I'm mad at him because after he took a call while on our date, he left me at the restaurant to go back to work. He didn't even take me home, he called me a cab. And stuck me with the bill."

Meredith walked over to Tayla and slid in beside her to give her a hug. "I'm sorry it's not the engagement ring you had hoped for. But you need to forgive him. He explained the job to you. He's a doctor, he has no choice. He has to be available, twenty-four seven."

"You're right, but--"

"I'm totally on your side. I wouldn't want to be left at the restaurant and certainly wouldn't want to be stuck with the check, but to ruin what you have because of something out of his control? Are you sure you want to do that?"

"Don't you think he should have called me to apologize?"

"Absolutely. And he was wrong in the way he handled everything. But he probably doesn't know you're upset. He left before he saw your reaction. To him, it was a lovely dinner followed by his job interrupting things. You need to call him. Patch things up. Don't let this ruin your relationship."

"Wow. Where's this pro Bennett coming from? You haven't been his biggest fan."

"Look, you know how I feel about him, but his job shouldn't be the reason you break up."

"Seriously?"

"Call him."

"I—"

Meredith handed Tayla her phone. "If you don't want to talk, send him a text. Baby steps."

Before she changed her mind, she sent Bennett a text. Seconds later, Bennett texted back.

#

Before lunch, they knocked out three sections of the display. Now, after lunch, they revisited them. Dene thought about the display at lunch and thought it would flow better if they moved it around. After hearing his ideas, both Tayla and Meredith agreed. It looked like it would be another late night, especially since Zet and Shalhoub didn't return after lunch.

Two hours later, Meredith's phone rang. "What?... No, I'll be right there. ...Okay. Hospital instead. ...I'm on my way."

Before Meredith could say anything, Tayla said, "Go. Call and fill me in on the way."

Meredith hugged her, grabbed her bag, and ran out the door.

"What is wrong?" Dene asked.

"I'll let you know as soon as she calls with details."

It seemed like hours passed before Meredith called.

"Her brother was in an accident. Cuts and bruises, hit his head. They want him to be checked, just in case. They are taking him to Mercy."

Tayla fished through her purse for her phone and called Bennett.

"Hey. I—They are taking Meredith's brother to the emergency room. ... Can you? ... Thank you. ... Talk to you later."

"Are you okay?"

"Yes. Let's keep going. We have a lot to get done."

Tingles shot up Tayla's arms. Sweat trickled down her back. The smell of Dene's cologne excited her. She went to the other side of the room to get away from him. Why did he make her feel this way?

Tayla kept looking at her phone. Still no news on Meredith's brother. A couple hours passed, her phone beeped, and a pop-up message appeared on the screen. After reading it, she filled Dene in. "Meredith said her brother is fine. He has a slight concussion. She is staying with him tonight and taking tomorrow off."

"That is good news. Glad he is going to be okay."

He smiled at her and she felt her cheeks heat up.

They worked on the exhibit another five hours before Tayla declared time to call it for the day. "Go ahead and go. I'll finish closing up. Besides, I parked on Schenley because of the game. I want to wait until the crowd dies down before I leave."

"I would be happy to escort you to your car, "

"That's okay. You don't have to wait. I can always have security escort me."

"You have been here all day. You need your rest as well. I will walk you to your car. It would be my honor."

"Thank you." She shoved her sketches into her bag and walked to the door. Dene followed, hurrying around her to open the door for her. She switched off the light and after they were in the hall, she made sure to pull the door tight, listening to it click and testing the handle to check the lock. Then she turned to Dene. "Are you sure you don't mind walking me to my car?"

His turquoise eyes twinkled. "I do not mind. You should not be out alone at night."

Tayla couldn't explain it, but she felt a connection to Dene, like she'd known him all her life. He excited her and made her feel — special? But yet so much more than special. She didn't want their walk to end. She could feel her face getting hotter, could feel her heart beating faster and knew her ears were burning.

The wind picked up and a light rain started to fall. She shivered and rubbed her arms for warmth.

"Where are my manners?" He took off his jacket and draped it over her shoulders.

"Thank you." His cologne enveloped her — earthy, anise, and something else she couldn't quite place. She closed her eyes and breathed in his scent. So familiar, but nothing commercial. She inhaled again, awash in the smell of him, yet feeling it wasn't close enough.

She blinked and shook herself aware. "We're almost there. I'm ahead in the garage on the right. Thank you. I really appreciate it, and I owe you."

"You do not owe me. I enjoyed the company."

She pointed to her car. "That's me. Thank you again for walking me to the car. Can I give you a lift somewhere?" Tayla used her fob to unlock the car. They both reached for the handle at the same time, and his hand brushed hers. Her hand shook, partly from the awkwardness of the moment and partly from the sudden rush of desire she was feeling. She dropped her keys.

They reached for them at the same time, and their hands touched again. She sucked in a breath and exhaled slowly, the keys all but forgotten. Her cheeks grew even hotter as she felt warmth suffusing her belly, curling lower, suggesting lascivious possibilities.

She glanced into his turquoise eyes, flicked a look over his entire body. She noticed the muscles in his arms jumped, and with his cologne tickling her senses, she realized how much she wanted him—all of him—caressing her, kissing her, exploring her secrets.

Her body shook with both a little fear of uncertainty and desire as she moved closer to him. She leaned into him against the car and slid her hands up to his collar. Before she changed her mind, she softly ran her tongue over his lips, gently exploring until her restraint faltered, then crushed her mouth to his. Nothing prepared her for the passionate feelings that overtook her. She pulled back. Her body ached and her heart pounded with need. She gasped for air.

He reached for her again, wrapping his arms around her, pulling her back into the shelter of his arms. She leaned against him when he brushed his lips against her neck. Tayla tilted her head back as Dene began tracing her neck with delicate kisses. The anticipation burned her alive from the inside—she trembled in his arms. She wanted him. Now.

He mimicked her original kiss, following the outline of her lips with his tongue. Unable to deny gratification any longer, she covered his mouth with hers in a passionate kiss—deeper and more searching than the first kiss. A kiss like this was a promise of much more to come.

Tayla broke the kiss. "Oh, oh, I shouldn't have done that. Forgive me—that was unprofessional and inappropriate. And I'm in a relationship." She handed him his jacket, got in her car, and drove off.

Michele Jones

CHAPTER FIVE

What is he doing? Why is he with her? He needs to focus on Meredith. If he ruins this for me …

Zet made his way to the museum. Meredith was the queen. She would be the one to break the curse. He had a plan, and if Dene stopped following it…

Time for him to take action. No more straying from his plan. Five days have passed and time was running out.

Zet summoned Dene to him. "I know you were with Tayla, and I am not pleased. You need to focus on Meredith. She is my queen. She is the one that shall free me."

"Do you not mean that she is your chance at being released from the curse?"

Zet wondered how much Dene knew. Was he making it difficult on purpose? Maybe he didn't want Zet to be free. No, Zet wouldn't let him ruin his chance. He must push Dene toward Meredith. She was the one that would break that insufferable curse.

"Speak not to me in that tone. I am your king and will not be disrespected."

"You are right. My apologies, my king."

"That is much better. Now, listen to me. We must both pursue Meredith. She is the one. Look closely at her. She looks quite like my queen—her skin, amber hair. That girl is the one." And the key to breaking this insufferable curse.

"So, Meredith is the one. Like Charlotte in London. But don't forget, she wasn't interested in me. Just what I could give to her. "

"Charlotte adored you. You didn't give her a chance." Zet saw Dene roll his eyes.

"I am sorry. I do not see it that way. Remember Quetzalxochitl, the Aztec Queen?"

"Yes. She was perfect for you. I saw the way she looked at you."

"She wanted me as a human sacrifice. She tied me to a sacrificial stone and was preparing to cut my heart out."

"But she didn't. You are making this much more difficult than it should be. Quetzalxochitl was not the only woman I found for you."

"Are you speaking of Ming Lei? The ancient Chinese warrior princess. She also wanted to kill me."

"You just didn't give her a chance."

"The twins. Filippa and Ladonna?"

"They both wanted you. You should have taken them both. I would have."

"I do not need your help. I am capable of finding the one. The queen. The woman that will free us both."

"If I do not find her first."

"We lived in Egypt for centuries, not one girl pleased you. We have been around the world, and returned to my native home. Still you found no one. I have tried, but none of the women I found was my queen. But several women wanted you. They must be the queen reincarnate. My queen was attracted to you. That attraction cursed you, now you do not search for her."

"The women you found were never about me. They were always about you, your happiness, your freedom. You never cared whether they truly made me happy, you only wanted someone to release you from the curse."

"The curse was very clear. Pass the tests that are needed to get into the afterlife, culminating with the weighing of the heart, or one of us finds and wins the reincarnated queen's heart. The tests are stacked against me. My only chance is for one of us to win the hand of the reincarnated queen."

"I cannot believe you. You do not care about me or the queen. The only thing you care about is you. And being freed from the curse.

"Enough." Zet's voice boomed and echoed through the small room. "You will stop this nonsense with that Tayla girl. She is not the one, not the queen. I have found the one. Meredith. I am trying, but should she not come to me, you must try, too. She is someone that could make you happy. Look closely at Meredith. You will see that she bears the tattoo of my queen on her left shoulder. She was my queen, the woman that gave you true happiness. She is the one to free us both from this half existence."

Dene sighed. "Perhaps I must give her more of a chance. I will try harder, my king. But you must try, too."

"I am trying, you fool."

"Not with the girl. With your lessons. To pass the weighing of the heart ceremony."

Rage coursed through Zet's veins. "I said I was trying! How dare you question me?"

"Of course, my king. What was I thinking?"

"Be gone." Zet waved him away.

Zet watched as Dene left. He didn't know the truth. He would never have the queen. He kept Dene from her before, and he would keep them apart again. He only needed to believe he had found her. As long as his heart was committed, that should be enough to end the curse. The gods would not know the difference.

The gods Anubis, Isis, and Osiris appeared before him.

"Do not forget your true quest," they spoke in unison. "Learn from your mistakes. Finding the queen is not your main directive."

"You will not—"

Zet spun around the room, but saw no one. It must be the curse. The gods would never speak to him as such.

CHAPTER SIX

Dene walked back to his room. It was only a few blocks from the museum, but it gave him time to think. He closed his eyes and pulled on his jacket to shield him from the cold misty rain. Tayla's kiss, still fresh, lingered on his lips. Something about her drew him to her, but he couldn't quite place it.

Zet's words echoed in his head. Meredith flashed before his eyes. Could she be the one? She appeared exactly like his lover, MerNeith. The hair, the eyes. Even the same tattoo. His heart even fluttered when they first met in the crowded hall at the museum.

Why was this so difficult? It should not be. Tayla had a boyfriend, Meredith did not. The first day he met them, both girls made him feel something that he hadn't felt in millennia—the desire to find happiness. Each girl gave him something special— they made him smile, and they also made him nervous.

Dene rubbed the coin in his pocket and then pulled out his key. He went inside and changed out of his wet clothes. Nothing in this room belonged to him. Even the clothes he wore weren't his, and they didn't fit him properly. He needed to go shopping. If he wanted to pull off this identity, he needed clothes that fit—among other things.

After a hot shower, he pulled out the laptop. A few clicks of the mouse and he found the nearest shopping center, Ross Park Mall. How convenient to have a place that one could go to purchase clothing. He had never worried about that when he had been alive. A loin cloth had sufficed. But now, in all these new existences, appropriate attire had become an issue. Tomorrow he would go to the shopping place, but tonight he needed to rest.

Both girls filled his head—Meredith, the one that looked like his lover, and Tayla, the one that kissed him so passionately. Perhaps after he slept, he could make a better decision. He made his way to the bedroom and surveyed his surroundings. Nothing here reminded him of home. How did Shalhoub live like this?

He didn't know why, but he wished he had something other than his coin to remind him of home. The crypt had a few of his belongings, but he could not take them from the display. Besides, he had nowhere to keep them. If he needed to see them, he would visit the display. This half-life gave him nothing. It provided him necessities, but not the important things. No friends, no family, no home.

After closing the blinds, and the covering that topped them, he crawled into bed. He was exhausted. He dreamt of his lover and the way she made him feel. He remembered the exact way she slid her hands over his chest, and how his body responded, how he ached for her to continue. How his skin tingled at her touch. His body betrayed him, and he reacted to her memory. The way she moved, the subtle flirting, the sly smile. He ached to be with her.

He tossed fitfully. He looked into her eyes, and his breathing quickened. His lover wrapped her arms around him and his muscles tightened, responding to her. As he breathed her in, she brushed his lips with hers, teasing and then pulling away. She traced his lips with her fingers and then pressed her mouth on his. His entire body gave in, and he moved them carelessly down to the blankets. MerNeith's face turned into Tayla's face.

Dene bolted straight up. Not only had his lover invaded his dreams but so had Tayla. He got out of bed and paced the room. He needed to relax. He tried going back to bed. He closed his eyes, but continued tossing and turning, sleeping on and off, dreaming of his former lover, and the kiss from Tayla. When he looked at the bedside clock again, it read 6:42. Why was Tayla invading his dreams? Maybe a cold shower would help?

It didn't.

#

Dene grabbed Shalhoub's keys. He had to get out of there. Thank the gods, he learned to drive when he was last alive. Before Dene pulled out of the parking garage, his phone rang. It was Tayla. A knot formed in his stomach. He did not know what to say to her. He ignored the call.

After fighting traffic, he arrived at the mall. Another concrete jungle that had to be navigated. Cars packed every isle and the large building looked cold and uninviting.

Dene parked as far from the building as he could. The crisp air helped him clear his head. Meredith and Tayla still clouded his mind. He felt a connection to both. And he thought Tayla had connected with him. The way she looked at him with those piercing green eyes. They held a secret. And her smile. It could stop the Nile. She intrigued him. They had nothing in common, and she had a boyfriend. She wasn't the one for him. Perhaps Zet was right. Meredith could be the one to break the curse. To give him the peace he needed to cross to the afterlife.

Zet's words clouded his mind. His thoughts turned to Meredith. That creamy skin and auburn hair, she looked just like MerNeith. The way she moved — so smooth, so effortless. The way she put him at ease when they first met. Her face clouded his vision, and before he knew it, he bumped smack into the woman in front of him.

"Please, accept my apology," Dene said. "I wasn't watching where I walking."

"No problem," she said.

"Meredith?" Dene asked.

"Dene. What are you doing here?"

"Ah. Er. The airport lost my luggage. I need to purchase more clothing. I only have a few pieces that I keep in my travel bag."

"That sucks. Do you want some company? I had to get out of the hospital for a while. I just can't sit there doing nothing."

"Forgive me, where are my manners? How is your brother doing?"

"He's going to be fine. I'm there more for my parents than for my brother. He was lucky. His concussion test came back negative. The doctor is keeping him overnight as a precaution. Other than that, there's nothing they can do for him."

"That is excellent news. I am pleased that he is doing well."

"I have some time before I need to get back. Let's get you some clothes."

Meredith took Dene into Hollister to get him some casual clothes. She handed him an assortment of jeans, oxford shirts, khakis, and polos.

"I am not sure about this."

"Trust me. These are the latest style," Meredith replied. "Try them on. You'll thank me later."

Dene went into the dressing room to try on his things. He stripped to his boxers and stepped into a pair of pants. He found them to be tight, and low on his waist, and torn in the knees.

"Dene, what's taking you so long? Come out and let me see them on you."

"These denim pants are defective. They have holes in the knees."

Meredith laughed, "They're supposed to be that way, come out and let me see."

Dene didn't move.

"I'm waiting."

He could not possibly wear these in public. People would talk. He would try on the other clothes. He unbuttoned the jeans, and the door opened.

"What are you doing? Those jeans look great on you. Why didn't you come out?"

"I—I cannot wear these. They do not fit properly."

"They fit fine, now finish trying everything on, and we'll get you something less casual."

Dene waited for her to leave. She resembled his lover in many ways, but he felt nothing. Why? She reminded him of a good friend, not his lover. Perhaps he did not give her a chance. He would try harder.

After several wardrobe changes, he chose a few items, including the denim pants that Meredith had chosen for him.

Dene and Meredith spent the next two hours shopping. They walked from store to store holding hands, talking and laughing.

It felt nice to have someone to talk to other than Zet, someone he considered a friend.

"I'm having a great time, but I need to get back," Meredith said.

"I am sorry, I did not mean to keep you so long," Dene replied.

"You didn't. I'm glad that I could help."

"It would be my pleasure to walk you to your car." Dene offered her his arm.

"Well, this is my car." Meredith unlocked it and waited by the door.

Dene opened it for her. "Thank you for shopping with me. You have helped me acquire some great clothing."

Meredith slid into the driver's seat. "I'm glad I ran into you. It was nice to take my mind off my brother for a while." She closed the door, started the car, waved to him, and pulled out.

Dene waved goodbye. He walked to his car more confused than before. He did not feel anything for Meredith. He rubbed the coin in his pocket. He needed to talk to a friend, not Zet.

CHAPTER SEVEN

Who could that be? Meredith wasn't coming over until later. "Coming." Tayla wrapped herself in her robe before going to the door. She looked out the window. What in the… ? She couldn't believe…

She opened the door. "Bennett, what are you doing here?"

"I can't believe you forgot. We have a date tonight."

She stood in front of the door, keeping him from entering. "We haven't spoken since you left me at the restaurant. I texted you, you sent a one-line reply and didn't reach out to me. Why would you think I would go out with you tonight?"

"Aren't you going to let me come in?"

Tayla turned and walked back to the couch.

"Honestly, Tayla. I can't believe you're upset. I had to leave, that's part of being a doctor, being on call. Get dressed. I'm taking you to Zia's."

"I have plans."

"It doesn't look like you're going anywhere."

"I was just going to get ready when you showed up."

He rolled his eyes. "I wanted to spend my only day off this month with you."

"You should have called."

"I was so busy at work, the time got away from me. I worked until midnight or later every night, I didn't want to wake you."

Maybe I should give him another chance. I may have been too hard on him. She shook her head. *He is a doctor. They do need him.*

"I would have understood. We're in this together."

"I'll do better."

"Promise?"

He crossed his heart. "Promise."

Five years is a long time. Can he really change? Should I go with him?

"Give me a—"

"Where's your ring? I thought you'd be wearing it."

"It doesn't exactly go with sweats." Tayla sighed. Maybe she should forgive him. "Give me a minute to change."

"What about your plans?"

"I'll deal with them."

"Mm-hmm."

Jerk. She swapped her sweats for jeans, and her cami for a sweater. After several unsuccessful hair style tries, she gave up and knotted it in a bun. Before she returned, she slipped the ring into her purse.

"You look fantastic." He made his way to her, and pulled her so close that she could feel his heart pounding.

She backed away, "I just need to grab my coat, and I'll be ready." He didn't seem disappointed by her lack of affection. A small frown creased her brow. She grabbed her phone and waved it in the air. "Canceling my plans." She sent Meredith a quick text. *Change of plans, can't do tonight. Will make it up to you. XO*

Before she could put her coat on, he was beside her, helping her. He could be so charming. He escorted them to the door, holding it open for her. This was one of those little things he did that had made her fall in love with him, but at the moment, it just irritated her.

Bennett took her hand and walked her to his car. His hand was so soft, and so warm. She missed that. But lately, something about him was off. He worked all the time. He used to call her every day, at least four times, but lately, they barely spoke. Not even a text.

They lost something. The spark was missing. The magic was gone. Maybe tonight would be different.

Did she give in too quick? Should she have made him work harder for their date?

They made small talk on the way to Zia's. Once they were inside, the waiter recognized them and led them a cozy table for two in the back of the restaurant, away from the crowd.

Before the waiter left, Bennett asked for a bottle of the house wine, two salads, and ordered their favorite pizza. Hand tossed, light sauce, pepperoni, green olive, sausage, and hot peppers.

Bennett slid closer after the waiter left. He flashed her his dazzling smile, the one he used on her the first day they met. Those dimples used to make her heart flutter, now they were just ordinary. She sighed.

She couldn't help it, she leaned into his chest. It used to feel so good, so comfortable. Now, it just felt… she couldn't put her finger on it. Their relationship used to be so easy, so right. Another sigh. She closed her eyes, and Dene's face invaded her thoughts. She pulled away and sat straight up. This couldn't be happening. What was going on? Why was she seeing Dene?

"Are you okay?"

" Excuse me, I'll be right back." Tayla grabbed her purse and ran to the ladies' room. She slammed the door shut, threw her purse on the counter, and splashed cold water on her face. She couldn't believe Dene invaded her thoughts. That damn kiss. Why did she have to kiss him? And why couldn't she get it out of her mind? She couldn't be interested in him. Tayla had only turned to him in a moment of weakness. And now she couldn't get him out of her mind.

The door knob jiggled. Someone pounded at the door. "Are you done in there?" The voice was angry. She must have been in there longer than she thought.

Tayla looked in the mirror, fixed what little makeup she had on, smoothed her sweater, opened the door, and walked back to the table. She no sooner sat down, when the waiter returned carrying their salads and a basket of fresh bread.

Bennett poured them both another glass of wine and reached for the bread.

"You didn't call or text," Tayla said.

"Not this again." He wiped his mouth and took a sip of wine. "I told you, it's been a busy week, and I just didn't have the time. Now I do. Let's enjoy tonight."

"You left me at the restaurant."

"I'm here now."

"Until you get another call."

"Tayla. Baby. I had no choice. You know how important you are to me. And the Chief of Staff said I deserve time off. So you don't have to worry. You have me all night."

She knew his schedule would be unpredictable. But last Saturday should have been something special. Instead, it drove a wedge between them, and he didn't see it. Maybe she overreacted. Maybe she let it get to her, or she was being over-sensitive. But there was just something about their special date last week. It nagged at her, but she couldn't understand why.

"Is everything okay?" the waiter asked.

"Fine," they answered at the same time.

"Can I get you anything?"

"Some extra napkins and another bottle of wine, but don't make a special trip."

Bennett looked at his watch again.

"Why do you keep checking your watch?"

"We've been in here for a while, and I don't want to get a parking ticket."

"You should go feed the meter. The pizza should be here by the time you get back."

He leaned over and gave her a peck on the cheek. "I'll be right back."

#

As Bennett shoved quarters into the meter, a woman came up to him and gave him a big hug.

"Hey, sweetie."

"Mia, what're you doing down here?" Bennett asked.

"I'm headed to Sal's for a fitting. Where are you going?"

He put his arm around her and lead her away from Zia's. "I have a dinner meeting in a couple minutes."

"Let's grab a drink before your meeting."

"Honestly, I don't have the time."

"That's not what you said last night," she teased.

"Okay, but only one. Then I've got to get to my meeting."

He led her down the block into the Tattooed Monk, and to a seat at the far end of the crowded, dark bar. He ordered her a Bloody Mary and a club soda for himself.

Bennett looking at his watch. "I'm sorry, baby, I've got to get to my meeting." He threw a twenty on the bar to cover their drinks.

Before he could leave, she kissed him passionately on the lips. "Just a taste of what's to come."

#

Tayla looked at her watch. Five minutes passed since the Bennett went to feed the meter. What was taking him so long? Tayla threw her napkin on the table and went to the door. She looked outside but didn't see Bennett anywhere. She made her way back to their table.

As she sat down the waiter came with their order. He served a slice to Tayla and put one on a plate for Bennett. "Do you need anything else right now?"

"No, thank you." She waited another five minutes. Bennett still hadn't returned. She nibbled at the pizza on her plate. Tayla checked her watch again, another five minutes had passed. She served herself another slice of pizza. It was getting cold. More time had passed, and her irritation level grew. Where was he?

Tayla went to the door again, but still saw nothing. She went back to the table and ate some more, noticing that she ate half the pizza. Their waiter stopped by the table to check on her. "Would you bring the check please?"

Moments later, he appeared with the check. "I'll take that for you when you're ready." He started to walk away.

"Wait," she called out as she dug her card out of her wallet. "Here you go."

He returned with her copy of the bill and a carry out box. "It will be just a moment, and I'll have this packaged and ready to go."

"Don't worry about it." Tayla turned and headed toward the door. Before she left she paused to speak with a few friends. After saying her goodbyes, she reached for the handle just as Bennett pushed it open and ran in.

"Tayla, where are you going? We haven't eaten yet."

"You haven't eaten yet. I'm finished.

"I don't understand."

"You've been gone for at least forty-five minutes. I couldn't wait any longer. I ate and paid the bill. I'm leaving."

"It wasn't gone that long. Dr. Williams stopped me on the street to ask my opinion about something. I answered him, put money in the meter, and I'm back.

"That's twice you left me at a restaurant." She pushed passed him and stomped out the door.

"Tayla, at least let me take you home," Bennett said."

"I don't need a ride." She called over her shoulder, never breaking stride. She kept walking.

Michele Jones

CHAPTER EIGHT

Something nagged at him. Dene paced his room and reflected about meeting Meredith at the mall. Although she looked like MerNeith—his queen, his lover—he didn't feel the familiar attraction. She reminded him of a close friend, someone fun to be around, but not his lover. She had to be the one. What had changed after all this time?

Zet was convinced that she was the one. The woman who could be his happily ever after. He laughed. The last few awakenings, Zet would tell him anyone could be the one. It didn't matter who she was or what she looked like. But if Meredith could be the one, he needed to give her a fair chance, especially since Zet had been pursuing her. To be free of the curse and find happiness after searching for thousands of years—especially with

MerNeith—he deserved that. Could she be interested in him? But what about the kiss Tayla gave him.

That kiss. His mind went back to that kiss. He could still feel the heat. Sparks flew. Even now his heart beat faster as he thought about it, and it made his palms sweat—again. Tayla's kiss made him feel something he hadn't felt in millennia.

The doorbell rang, pulling him back into the present, and he rose to answer it. "Meredith? Is everything okay?"

"Yes, everything's fine. I just left the hospital and thought since you live close by, you might want to grab a bite to eat at the new club downtown."

A voice echoed in Dene's head. She could be the one. He motioned her inside. "Thank you for thinking of me. I would love to. Excuse me while I get ready."

After a quick change into the jeans that Meredith helped him purchase and a splash of cologne, he returned, ready to go out.

"I told you those jeans looked great on you."

Dene felt his cheeks grow hot and he tugged at his waistband. "Thank you, you are too kind." Then took her by the arm and they headed out.

#

"Dene, I'm so glad you wanted to come. I've been dying to go to Nebula. Everyone just raves about it."

"Thank you for inviting me, this looks like a fine establishment." Dene rubbed the coin in his pocket. He reached around and put his arm behind Meredith's back to lead her inside. The place was crowed, and the music boomed in his head. A scantily clad woman came up to them and took their names.

"The wait shouldn't be too long." She pointed to another room. "You're welcome to enjoy a drink and an appetizer at the bar while you wait."

Dene followed Meredith as she made her way to the bar. Inside, the music blared even louder, making his head hurt. It never ceased to amaze him how much things had changed in all his years.

All the tables were full at first glance. As they headed to the back of the room, Meredith kept stopping to talk with people she knew. She introduced him to each of her friends, made small talk, then moved to the next table. Suddenly she froze.

"Is something wrong?"

"That's Tayla's boyfriend, Bennett. You remember her talking about him." She pointed to a table tucked in a corner covered by hanging plants. "And he's not with Tayla. Let's go talk to him."

Before Dene could protest, Meredith headed toward him, grabbing his hand and pulling him along.

"Bennett, what are you doing here?"

Bennett stood. "Meredith."

"I thought—"

"This is Dr. Coldwell. She is consulting with me on a particularly difficult case. Who's your friend?"

"Sorry. This is Dene, he is working on the museum exhibit with Tayla and me."

Bennett extended his hand. "Nice to meet you." He turned to Meredith. "Please excuse us. Dr. Coldwell only has an hour, and I need her assistance."

"It was a pleasure to meet you as well. We shall leave you alone." Dene slid his hand into Meredith's and led her to an empty table nearby.

"That was awkward."

"Why?"

"Tayla usually goes out with Bennett every Saturday. I thought she was going out with him tonight. Instead he's here. With a colleague. Honestly, he should be with Tayla."

"We should not judge. Perhaps something came up." A twinge of jealousy hit him. Could that man really be Tayla's lover? He just didn't seem to be her type. She was so kind and feeling. He seemed cold and uncaring. Perhaps it was the healer in him.

He remembered her kiss and lost awareness of everything else.

"Let's order something," Meredith said. Her words shook him out of his reverie. "I'm starving."

They ordered drinks and made small talk while they waited for a table. It wasn't long before the hostess called them.

Dene rose, walked around the table, and helped Meredith with her chair. He smiled at her and wrapped his arm around her waist. She did look like his lover. And he was trying. Why didn't he feel the excitement? He reached his hand into his pocket and rubbed his coin. Something didn't feel right. He couldn't place it, but something was off.

They had barely finished dinner when Meredith grabbed his hand and led him to the dance floor. "I just love this song."

He stood and watched as she danced beside him. He was completely out of his element.

"Come on, loosen up."

"I—I do not dance."

She moved closer to him and danced around him, putting her hands on his hips, swaying them to the music. "See, you can dance. Now just relax and follow what I do."

Sweat rolled down his face. He jammed his hands into his pocket and rubbed his coin. He started to move his feet. He was clumsy at first, but he got better. He put a little distance between them, so he wouldn't hit her when he moved, but she moved closer. The music stopped.

"I'm going to slow it down a bit for all you lovers out there," the DJ announced.

Meredith grabbed Dene and pulled him to her. She put his hands on her hips and wrapped her hands around his neck as the music started. Within seconds, she had her head resting on his chest. The feeling was nice but didn't make his heart race. He just couldn't figure it out.

Before the song ended, someone tapped him on the shoulder. Zet.

"May I cut in?

Dene stepped back, glad for the reprieve. "Meredith, I'll be at our table."

Damn that curse. It gave Zet the ability to track him. Zet better not hurt her. The way he pursued her, she must be the queen.

Dene believed he should protect Meredith. Zet used people. He would use Meredith as a means to an end. Then what? Dene tried to fall in love with Meredith, but all he felt was affection. Still, that didn't mean he wanted her to get hurt. And he knew if Zet pursued her, she would get hurt. He took his seat, sipped his drink, and kept his gaze trained on his king.

Meredith and Zet made their way to the table after the dance ended. She looked like she was having a good time. Dene flagged down a waitress and ordered a round of drinks. It was shaping up to be a long night.

#

Dene awoke with a pounding headache. Last night came back to him in pieces. First Meredith showing up, inviting him to dinner. Then drinking those, those margaritas—he believed that was what Meredith called them. She warned him to take it easy on them. But he did not listen because they tasted excellent and he liked how they made his head buzz. After several icy beverages, dinner finally arrived, and his head stopped buzzing. He remembered her pulling him onto the dance floor and teaching him to dance. Then Zet showed up. So he went back to the table and had more of those delicious green drinks.

The room spun when he closed his eyes. He had never experienced anything like that before. He couldn't move without the room spinning. What was happening? His mouth felt like sandpaper and he needed water. Once the room-spinning slowed, he carefully put his feet down and headed to the kitchen. Even the floor spun. No more icy green margaritas for him.

Before he got to the kitchen, his phone rang. The ringing pounded in his head. He rushed as fast as he could to the phone to make it stop.

"Hello."

"Hi, Dene," Meredith said. "Just calling to see how you are this afternoon."

Must she scream into the phone? Afternoon? Had he actually slept that long?

"I'm fine. Thank you for asking. But I must go. I have an appointment that I must keep. I will see you tomorrow."

He ended the call, grabbed his head, and flopped on the couch. His stomach felt queasy. Dene couldn't move without the room spinning, his mouth was dry, and he slept half the day. He even had the same clothes on from the night before.

Dene massaged his temples before getting off the couch. He needed that water. Before he could get to the kitchen, Zet materialized in front of him.

"Why are you not ready? We have work to do. It is time for my next lesson. And we need to continue our search."

Gods, he wished he had the power to dematerialize Zet instead of the other way around.

#

Dene already wasted the first half of the day. Now the second half of his day would be spent teaching Zet what he needed to know to pass the test, and helping him continue his search. Today, he wouldn't get anything accomplished for himself. The coin in his pocket should be smooth from all the rubbing he had been doing lately.

He was in no mood or shape for Zet today. The searching and working on his manners necessary to pass the next test would take a lot out of him. Zet could not care less about the gods or the curse they placed upon them. He only cared about knowing enough to fool the gods. Did he actually believe that the gods would be fooled? If he did, he was mistaken.

Not only did Zet demand his help and knowledge to pass the test, he commanded his time. While he spent time helping Zet, he didn't have time to search for his queen — his true love, the reason for his cursed existence.

"Dene, we need to get started now. If you cannot handle the late nights with Meredith, then you must stay home. Completing our tasks is the only thing that is of importance. Besides, she is not interested in you. She prefers me. Did you not see the way she looked at me last evening?"

His remarks struck a nerve, and Dene furiously rubbed the coin in his pocket. He set his jaw and turned to Zet. "We shall see."

"She looks like my queen, does she not? You do not stand a chance. She was mine before and she shall be mine once again. Now, let us begin the lesson."

Even though his feelings were not as strong for Meredith as they were for his queen, Zet was right — she looked just like her.

Could he really make this work between them? She appeared to be attracted to him. Did she recognize him even though the curse was to keep her from knowing? If she did, that could be why she wanted to be around him.

CHAPTER NINE

Tayla was livid. Last night was a total failure. For the second time in two weeks, Bennett left her at the restaurant — with the bill. Last week, the date started out promising, she even thought he was going to propose. Instead, he gave her an emerald ring — beautiful, but not a diamond—but rushed out because of an emergency, without taking her home.

This week he left to add money to the parking meter and was gone for almost an hour. She ate half a pizza pie and drank the second bottle of wine — alone. Even worse, she blew off Meredith to be with him.

Lately he just wasn't the same person she fell in love with. He still did the little things that made her fall in love with him, but he fell short on the big things. Why wasn't she important to him anymore? She wanted him to make her the most important thing in his world. He hadn't. She was second to everything else in his life. She knew being with a doctor would be challenging, but she hadn't expected to be completely ignored.

Her stomach felt queasy. Too much pizza and wine. She made her way to the medicine cabinet and grabbed some antacid. After downing them, she brewed herself a cup of espresso and slumped down at the kitchen table.

She went back to her kiss with Dene the other night. It was passionate, fiery, and made her blush. A kiss like that should be shared with her boyfriend, not with someone she barely knew.

Her cell phone buzzed, a text message from Bennett. She wasn't in the mood. It buzzed again, and again, and again. Did he really think she was going to speak to him? After last night? He was seriously mistaken. He had a lot of making up to do.

Ugh.

She tried to pull herself up, but couldn't. Her head throbbed harder and her legs were heavier than a single pyramid stone. Wincing, she tried again, this time making it to the couch. Something needs to give. Bennett either needed to make her his priority or she needed to move on to someone else. She closed her eyes and fell asleep.

The doorknob jiggled, awakening her from a fitful sleep.

She looked around the room for something she could use to protect herself. The only items in the room were a picture frame and several pillows. The pounding of her heart matched the pounding in her head. It intensified as the door knob turned.

Tayla grabbed her phone and dove behind the couch. Her head pounded harder with each movement, but she didn't want to be a sitting target. She managed to stifle a scream. The door opened, and in crept the intruder. She typed 9-1-1 on her keypad and was about to hit send.

"Tayla? Where are you?"

Tayla breathed a sigh of relief. Then she eased herself off the floor and back onto the couch. "Bennett. What are you doing here? How did you get in?"

"I used the key you keep outside in the flower box. When you didn't answer my texts, I thought something was wrong. I rushed over to make sure you were okay."

"I'm fine. Thanks for your concern. It's not your responsibility to check up on me. I didn't answer your texts because I didn't want to talk with you. Furthermore, you had no right to use that key. "

He sat beside her on the couch and put his arm around her shoulder. "What's bothering you?"

"You. Your lack of commitment to us. Your disappearance last night."

"You never gave me the chance to explain what happened."

"There's nothing to explain. You left me at Zia's. That's the second time in two weeks that you left me at a restaurant."

"Listen, baby. I didn't think I was gone that long. When I was putting the money in the meter, a colleague of mine flagged me down for my opinion. We started talking about the case. I answered the questions and came straight back—as you were leaving. Honestly, I thought I was only gone for a few minutes."

Tayla felt her cheeks heat up. "Bennett, your focus is everywhere but on our relationship. You ask me out for a special dinner, and I think it's because you want to marry me. I shouldn't have reacted the way I did, but I was hurt when you didn't propose."

"Baby, I didn't know you were ready for marriage. We never discussed it. I thought nice jewelry was the next logical step. Let's talk about it."

"I'm not in the mood for it. Actually, I'm not in the mood for anything right now. Leave."

Bennett took her hand in his. "Don't be like that. I'm here now. Tomorrow I have a full schedule."

She threw his hand off hers. "Not today. " She stood and winced.

"What's wrong? Let me look."

"Stop. I'm fine. "

"Tayla --"

"Enough. Leave. And give me that key. I can't do this now." Tayla grabbed his arm and pulled him to the door. She opened it and stood there with her arms crossed. "Leave. Now."

"I'll leave, but we were meant to be together. You'll see," Bennett said.

She slammed the door behind him.

Tayla paced the kitchen. How dare he come here and think he could smooth things over with a lame excuse?

#

Three aspirin, two cups of espresso, and one bag of M&Ms, and she still didn't feel better.

Her phone vibrated. Meredith wanted to do something.

Come over. We can watch a movie and chat. Walk in. The door will be open.

Thirty minutes later, the door opened. Meredith walked in carrying a huge bag of M&Ms and a large bag of chips.

"I've got something to tell you." Meredith said. She looked happy, almost glowing.

"Spill it."

"Well, when you canceled on me yesterday, I stopped at Dene's on the way home from the hospital."

"Oh, I'm sorry. How is your brother?"

"He's fine. They're planning to release him on Tuesday."

"That is good news. Sorry for interrupting. You stopped at Dene's?"

"Well, I was close, and I wanted to try that new place downtown, Nebula. So I invited him to go with me. And he said yes. I even got him to wear the new clothes I helped him pick out."

"You two went shopping?"

"Not really. I went to the mall, and he was there. So I volunteered to help him shop. Anyway, I asked him to wear the clothes I picked out for him—jeans and an oxford shirt. You know, he's built."

Tayla squirmed. "I hadn't noticed."

"Nebula was great. We were there for hours. Then Zet showed up. We danced, and talked. Spent half the night together. I think Zet likes me."

"Zet?"

"Yeah. Why?"

"Well, the way you were going on about Dene and shopping and his body…"

"Nah. We're just friends. I mean, the guy is good looking. But so what? Lots of guys are. I'm not blind."

"You're interested in Zet?"

Meredith munched on a pretzel. "He's good looking. Has a good body." She sighed. "And let me tell you, that man has some serious moves."

"Uhhh, that's great."

"What's wrong?"

"Nothing. I'm happy for you."

"I know you, Tay. Spill it."

"It's Bennett. We had another fight." She took the M&Ms and started sorting them—brown, red, yellow, orange, blue, green.

She grabbed a handful of the brown ones and popped them into her mouth. "That's all we seem to do lately."

"Tay, what happened?"

She kept eating the candies as she talked. "Last night, Bennett showed up to take me to dinner. I hadn't expected him, and when he showed up I was surprised so I decided to forgive him."

"And?"

"We went out. To Zia's. He ordered our favorite. He seemed to be the old Bennett.

"Tay—"

"The place was crowded. He didn't want to get a ticket, so he went out to feed the meter. He was gone almost an hour. I ate alone—again. I got tired of waiting, so I paid the bill and left. On my way out I ran into him coming back. He tried to explain, but I didn't give him the chance." She reached for the rest of the brown M&Ms.

"I'm so sorry."

"It's not your fault. I just don't understand it."

"Maybe I shouldn't say this, but Dene and I saw him at Nebula."

"What?"

"Maybe I shouldn't have said anything."

"Did you talk to him? What did he say?"

"Yes, I talked with him. He was there with a colleague. Said he was doing a consult and didn't have time to chat. Actually, he fluffed us off. I didn't think anything about it at the time, but—"

Tayla snagged the orange M&Ms. Her hands shook in anger. "I—That—He's such a—I can't believe he went out with someone else. Even if it was for a consult. I guess I just don't mean that much to him anymore."

"I don't think—"

Tears formed in the corners of her eyes. "We've been together for years. Honestly, I thought he was the one. Now, I'm not so sure. We just don't seem to be connecting."

"Maybe you need to give the relationship a time out. Think about what you want, then talk to him. Right now you're too emotional. Don't make any rash decisions that you'll regret."

"You're right. Thanks for coming over. Let's find a good comedy and change the subject."

Michele Jones

CHAPTER TEN

Dene slumped on the couch and rested. Working with Zet was always a challenge. He didn't listen and acted like he knew everything. They were on number forty-three. This would be the final lesson that he had to teach Zet. That meant this would be the last chance either of them had to find the queen and get her to commit to one of them. If he failed, the gods would force them to start over. More lessons. More searching. Neither of them had any luck so far. This damn curse. Every time they had found her, she hadn't recognized either one of them. Worse yet, the last time they found her, she had been more attracted to Zet.

He couldn't let that happen this time.

Now Zet was interested in Meredith. Her looks and the tattoo convinced him she was the queen reincarnated. Zet even showed up at Nebula and cut in on his time with her to try and curry her favor. Damn curse. He didn't know what worried him more, that he wasn't attracted to Meredith or that Zet was and that he'd hurt her for his own nefarious needs.

They were so close to the end. And this time... this time, it mattered.

He picked up the newspaper he bought earlier. It was filled with terrible things—murders, car accidents, death notices. Nothing good. His phone buzzed, but he chose to ignore it. He closed his eyes and drifted off to sleep.

#

MerNeith walked over and took his hand. "My king is lying with another. Follow me." She led him down the torch-lit corridor to her private chamber, where the moonlight illuminated the fruit and wine on the table and the pallet on the floor.

He caressed her cheek, then leaned in toward her and kissed her. His lips were gentle on hers, his breathing hard and fast.

She wrapped her arms around him and pulled them both down. The pallet cushioned them, the covers soft, her skin even softer. She massaged his shoulders and his arousal grew. He moved closer to her, removed her jeweled headdress and worked his hands down to her sheath. Her skin warmed under his fingertips, and he traced the linen neckline, skimming her throat and collarbone while playing with her necklace.

In mere seconds he undressed her, leaving only her jewelry. She lay next to him, her milky white skin and ornate jewelry reflecting in the light of the moon. Her soft sighs spurred him on as he caressed her firm, round breasts. He let his hands wander lower over her flat stomach, tracing patterns over her hips and thighs before parting her legs.

She moaned a soft sound of encouragement, arched her body toward his, and dug her nails into his back. They rolled together, and she pulled him on top of her. Her gasps grew to breathless pants, and she begged him to enter her.

He pressed his clothed form to her deliciously naked flesh, their bodies touching everywhere from heel to head, and he moved his hips against her to elicit more erotic moans from her. She was more than ready for him, he could feel her writhing beneath him, but he wanted to prolong her pleasure. He remained clothed, moving with her, teasing her to bring her to ever greater levels of desire.

His queen's hands roamed over the sensitive skin of his chest, rushing him toward a climax he wasn't ready for. He needed to slow things down. Dene rolled off her, smiled when she whined, and pinched her nipple. He took a fig from the table, dipped it in honey, and held it to her lips. She opened her mouth to receive the fruit and when she bit, the honey and fig juice trickled from her lips to her chin. Entranced by the shine of the fluid along her supple skin, Dene leaned in to trace the curve of her mouth with his own, first kissing her lips then licking down her chin to the graceful curve of her neck, sucking sticky sweetness from her.

The combined taste of her, the honey, and the fig spurred his lust.

Her eyes closed and she gave him a brief but naughty smile. When she opened her eyes, she reached for his hand and guided his fingers to her lips, placing soft kisses on his fingertips before inserting the digits into her mouth. She rolled each finger sensuously along her tongue and teeth while sucking them clean.

His body shuddered at the sensations, trembled at the thought of her doing that to other parts of his body.

She slid her hands under his shendyt kilt and massaged him.

He nearly bolted off the pallet.

"My queen." He could barely breathe. She teased him now, first caressing his thighs, then working her way to his groin. She teased him gently, and he moaned with pleasure at the sensation. Too soon the gentle fondling stopped, but before he could voice his displeasure, she wrapped her hand firmly around the base of his shaft, and a groan escaped him. She stroked him, bring him to the edge. Dene moaned as she stroked up the length of him, tracing her fingers over the wetness pooling at his tip, then dragged her wetted hand back down to his base once more. His control snapped.

He kissed her savagely. He traced her lips with his tongue while he reached to her parted legs with his hand and stroked her sex, his fingers mimicking his tongue. She spasmed at his touch. He claimed her mouth again and slid his fingers inside her, seeking her wetness until she opened to him, caressed her until she was on the brink of orgasm and begged him to slip inside of her.

Dene moved his hand beneath his kilt to position himself and then drove into her. His entry made her cry out, and he stilled. She shook her head violently and wrapped around him. He moved slowly at first, to be sure she could take it, but she bucked against him. He pounded into her at a thunderous pace, and she matched his rhythm, clawed at his back. She moaned in his ear and he whispered honeyed words back to her

Each thrust increased their pleasure, and he lifted his queen's legs higher, feeling her tightening along his length as he pushed deeper inside of her. Both of them increased their pace, pounding furiously against each other until he felt as though they became one. Dene felt his queen tightening around his shaft. As she cried out and with the first flutters of her orgasm, he violently thrust a few last times and began pumping his seed inside of her, and they finished beautifully together.

When his vision cleared, he brought her down gently until he fell limp beside her on the pallet. They lay together, wrapped in each other's arms, and minutes later, her rhythmic breathing told him she had fallen asleep.

The gods had truly blessed him. Dene closed his eyes and relived the moment. He pictured her black hair fanned out beneath her, her green eyes darkening then closing, her olive skin luminescent in the moonlight. One after another, the erotic images swam through his mind.

He bolted up, breathless. He wasn't thinking about his queen.

He was thinking about Tayla.

#

The alarm clock in the other room blared. Dene bolted straight up. He couldn't believe he slept the entire night on the couch, but his body told him otherwise. Stiff, cramped muscles. Everything ached. After a quick shower, he rooted in his refrigerator for food—he would eat on his way to the museum. No time to walk this morning. He would use the rental car.

A few minutes later, Dene made his way through security and up to the display. He was worried he would be the last one there, but he was first. He took the notes out of his bag and spread them across the table.

They had the display set up all wrong. Things needed to be moved. He stood and stretched, then decided to work on the *shabtis*. Shalhoub had put his *shabtis* far from the king. Zet would not be pleased. The *shabtis* were extremely important to the Egyptian pharaoh, they were the images of the workers and advisors that the pharaoh would need to help him in the afterlife. Ancient Egyptians believed as long as the dead person's name survived for posterity, they survived the afterlife. He worked on the plaque that would be displayed for them. The faces of the *shabtis* haunted him. Some were his friends. He recognized them, along with their names. He knew they made it to the afterlife. He could only hope that once he assisted Zet with his journey and taught him his lessons, he would be free to live out his earthbound life and in death proceed to the afterlife he deserved.

Shalhoub had the *shabtis*, along with the sarcophagi they had been place inside, shoved to a back corner of the room. These *shabtis* needed to be closer to the pharaoh. Each of them served a purpose. He had finished moving the last of the *shabtis* when the door opened. Shalom entered.

"Dene." Shalom nodded.

"Good morning, Siamun."

He backed away from Dene. "Where are the girls?"

"They haven't come yet. I have star—"

"What are these doing here? I'm sure I had them in the back. We need to feature the pharaoh, not the servants."

Dene crossed the room and stood in front of Shalhoub. "The servants are just as important as the king. As you know, in our culture, everyone serves a purpose. Without servants, the king could not possibly take care of himself in the afterlife. These servants were buried with him to cook, clean, plant, and do tasks that the king would never do for himself."

Shalhoub again backed away from Dene. "I don't think anyone today will care if the *shabtis* are not front and center. Return them where you found them."

"I will not. Our display will be authentic. These men and women devoted their lives for our king, and they deserve to be treated with respect. If you look closely, you will see their names and pictures on their sarcophagi," Dene said and moved closer to Shalhoub.

He knew he made Shalhoub uncomfortable. Zet was to blame for that. Perhaps he should try to sway him to his side. He was not the bad person here. Zet was.

"I would like to run an idea past you, Siamun."

"I'm listening," he said.

"I believe we should paint the far wall with the hieroglyphics found in the pyramid. We should put the address to the gods of the Taut. Perhaps we need to put that the dead needed to pass through a series of gates, each guarded by a demon, and the only way to pass was to name the demon and recite the proper spell."

"And I suppose you would do the painting?"

"I am sure I could help. You have some of the hieroglyphics, I have seen them."

Dene turned when the door opened. Meredith and Tayla came in.

"Sorry we're late," Meredith said. "There was an accident on the parkway. Let's get started."

"Did you move things before we came in?" Tayla asked.

"We did," Shalhoub said. "The *shabtis* shouldn't be buried in the back. They need to be with the Pharaoh, so I had Dene bring them to the front."

"I like it. It looks more authentic," Meredith said.

"Did you do anything else before we got here?" Tayla asked.

"Instead of painting all the walls, I would like to do hieroglyphics on the far wall. I think it will showcase the exhibit. We have some of ones from the pyramid, the rest we can recreate. And I know Dene has experience painting them."

They skipped lunch, working the entire day rearranging the exhibit.

"We need to call it a day," Tayla said. "Just leave what you are working on. We'll pick it up from there tomorrow."

"Does anyone want to get something to eat on the way home?"

"Dinner would be nice. We should all go out for dinner together. It would be nice to do something not work-related."

Tayla replied, "I'm in. How does Hello Bistro sound to everyone? They have the best burgers."

Before Shalhoub could say no, Dene put his hand on his shoulder. "Siamun, a word please?" Then he turned to the girls. "We shall meet you there."

"We'll save you a seat," Tayla said. "Don't be too long."

"We shall not," Dene replied.

#

After the girls left, Shalhoub threw Dene's hand from his shoulder. "Never touch me again."

"We must speak."

"We have nothing to discuss."

"We do. I believe the girls know that you do not care for me. I am not your enemy."

Shalhoub backed away from Dene. "You must be joking. You and that…that…mummy, er, pharaoh. You killed that guard. And you would have killed me as well if you didn't need me. Just stay away from me."

"I did not kill that guard, nor would I ever kill anyone. Zet is the evil one. I need you to believe me. If I were not tied to him by this curse, I would not be helping him."

"Everyone knows the curse. You have one of the most famous curses attributed to the ancient Egyptians. The pharaoh, the queen, and you were cursed to walk the earth to atone for your digressions. Once you have appeased the gods, they will grant you entrance to the afterlife."

"That is only part of the curse. Part of the hieroglyph missing."

"How convenient."

"You know I speak the truth. You have that broken hieroglyph in storage for the display. Are you not curious what is missing from it?"

"And I suppose you know what's missing?"

"I do. The missing piece states the king's salvation depends on me teaching him to be a better person. The last part of the curse involves finding the queen. The gods cursed her, and she does not know who we are. We must win her heart without her knowledge of either of us. The gods said she will commit to the one whose heart beats true. Whoever wins her heart gets to live out his life with her and be with her for all eternity. The other will continue on with the life that we are in at that time."

"No one has any knowledge of this. Why should I believe you?"

"I speak the truth. And I need your help. I cannot do this without you."

Dene rubbed the coin in his pocket. He could see Shalhoub trying to grasp what he had just learned. Had he been persuasive enough to win him over? Would he help him to win the queen?

"I… I don't know."

"I will be forever in your debt should you choose to help me."

"I don't know that I trust you, but I don't trust that mummy even more. So I'll help you on one condition. You promise me that neither you nor the mummy will harm my family."

"Agreed."

#

Dene and Shalhoub made small talk on the way to the restaurant. An uneasy feeling remained between them, but it waned slightly since their conversation.

"I'd like to know more about the curse. How exactly did you become entwined with Zet and the queen for eternity?"

Dene winced. He did not wish to discuss his personal life with Shalhoub, nor his intimacies. "It is a long story."

"I've got the time."

"Tonight, after we get home. I'll tell you everything."

Shalhoub stopped. "You'll tell me now, or I'm done helping you."

Dene sighed. "Zet was a terrible ruler. He cared naught for anyone, especially his sister, the queen. Once she gave him a son, he ignored her completely. We fell in love. Zet found out. When he died, he wanted us buried with him. Even though we no longer did that. The gods stepped in and spared my life, but with a condition. Zet was evil and couldn't enter the afterlife because he couldn't pass any of the forty-three judgments and the weighting of the heart, so I was tasked with teaching him. This was my punishment for having relations with the queen."

"That's some story."

"The truth can be very sorted."

"And what happens if he doesn't pass the judgments?

"We are at the restaurant."

"Tell me. What happens? Does he get to keep trying?"

"We get from solstice to solstice each century. If Zet cannot past the tests, we will go away and come back the next century to try again."

"And you have been trying to teach him for four-thousand years?"

"Yes, once each century for four thousand, three hundred years. Let's go inside. I will answer any other questions you have later." He held the door for Shalhoub.

The place was crowded for a weeknight. They looked around and spied the girls, and Zet waving to them from a booth in the back. "How fortunate for us they arrived here before us. Had they not, we might be waiting for a booth like the others."

Dene could not believe that Zet was there. Damn that curse. It gave Zet the ability to monitor his thoughts, track his whereabouts. Would his life ever be his own?

Dene looked around the place. He could not believe that so many people came to places like this to eat. They did not do these things in his time. So many things about this century surprised him—tight fitting clothes, telephones, music from a box. It was a lot to learn in such a little amount of time. Thank the gods they supplied the knowledge they did, especially the gift of tongues.

"We'll be right back," Meredith said.

"Where are you going?" Dene asked.

Neither girl answered, they just went down the hall.

"What did you and Shalhoub talk about on the way here? I know he does not trust us?"

"I tried to persuade him that we are not evil," Dene replied.

Zet turned to Shalhoub. "Does he tell the truth? Are you convinced that we are not evil, but rather just cursed?"

"I believe—" Shalhoub stopped when he saw the girls.

"So, what did we miss?" Tayla asked.

Meredith slid into the booth beside Zet, leaving the seat beside Shalhoub and Dene for Tayla. After the server came by and took their drink order, they grabbed the box on the table and started playing the trivia game against the other tables. Dene sat quietly, listening to them guess the answers.

"Feel free to answer at any time," Meredith said.

Dene tugged at his collar, then jammed his hands into his pockets and rubbed his coin. "I am happy watching."

"How sweet. We —"

"Sorry for the wait. Are we ready to order?"

Dene rubbed his coin harder. The attraction. The pull toward the queen. How had he missed it so many times before? Was she really sitting here? He could feel the passion, the longing. He felt it — sexual desire, stronger than ever.

CHAPTER ELEVEN

Tayla couldn't fall asleep. She could smell Dene's cologne and remembered the feel of his muscles straining through his shirt. Her attraction to him was greater than anything she felt in a long time. He clouded her dreams and invaded her senses when she was awake. Everything she did, every thought she had, he was there.

She tried soaking in a warm chamomile lavender bath with soothing music on the radio to relax her and help her sleep. Neither worked. She gave up, went to the kitchen, and made herself a snack. No use wasting this awake time. She would work on the hieroglyph that needed to be translated. Shalhoub had remarked that most of the pieces had finally been gathered. She overheard him say he hoped he would discover something about the pharaoh. Maybe this would give them a head start. If she lucked out, maybe the pieces would tell a story—give some insight on what really happened during his reign.

The hieroglyph made no sense. The pieces had not been assembled correctly, and there were gaps. Tayla shook her head. She tried cutting them out and moving them around. Still no luck. She shook her head and stifled a yawn.

For a few hours, she thought about translation and nothing else. She turned out the lights and went back to bed. Her head hit the pillow, and Dene crept back into her thoughts. She mentally shook her head. She was with Bennett. Kind of.

Tayla's alarm clock blared, piercing the silence like a hot poker. It made her head throb worse, and it was only 5:15. She silenced the alarm and pulled her pillow over her head. Last night's lack of sleep and her late dinner with Meredith and the guys contributed to a migraine.

Her cell phone text message went off, playing the same tone over and over. She reached out from under the blanket, her hand feeling the nightstand for her phone. Once found, she silenced it. Her head throbbed and her stomach felt queasy. Black spots clouded her vision. She made it to the bathroom just in time. Her stomach betrayed her. After purging, she washed up and grabbed her migraine medicine from the cabinet. She slumped against the sink, fumbling to get the bottle open. After several unsuccessful attempts, she managed to take two. Then she rested her head against the cool marble of the sink and held her stomach.

The pounding in her head was like a jackhammer breaking stubborn cement. Minutes passed before she could steady herself enough to make it back to bed. Tayla flopped down and massaged her head.

#

The pounding at the door woke her from a fitful sleep. Her meds kicked the migraine, but replaced it with a banging headache. She pulled the pillow around her ears. Maybe whoever was out there would give up and go away.

They didn't. The banging continued.

A muffled woman's voice took the place of the pounding. "Tay, are you all right?"

She winced and made her way to the living room. The door opened, and Meredith ran inside followed by Dene. Tayla grabbed the blanket from the back of the couch and covered up.

"Where have you been? I tried texting. I called. You didn't answer."

Tayla had slumped down on the couch. "Migraine."

"Oh, my God. I'm so sorry. When you didn't show, I thought something happened. The police came to the museum. They found Stan's body. And when you didn't show up, well, I thought… I needed to check to see if anything happened to you. I would have been here sooner, but my car's in the shop. I had to get a cab."

"I did not want her traveling alone," Dene said.

"Thank you, both."

Meredith pulled out her cell. "I'll call Bennett. He can come over and—"

"No! I don't need him to come over. I'm not in the mood to deal with him right now." Tayla noticed Dene pacing the room with his hands in his pockets. He looked—out of place.

"But he can prescribe you something for the migraine. You should let him help."

"It is my belief that Meredith is right. Let Bennett give you some relief from the pain. You should not have to suffer needlessly."

"I said no. I don't need his help."

"Fine. Be stubborn," Meredith said, jamming her hands on her hips. "Tell me, what can I do? Can I get you something?"

"I'll be okay. Don't worry. After a good sleep, I'll be ready to go. Please. Go back to work. I'll be in tomorrow."

"If you're sure you don't need me, er, us—"

"I'm sure. I don't need a babysitter. I just need to rest. Would you mind locking the door on the way out?"

#

Tayla stood in the shower and let the hot water run over her body. The pain in her head had eased into a dull throb. The warm water felt so good that she stood under the cascade until the water turned cold. She shivered and her stomach growled. She toweled off, threw on her sweats, and shuffled to the kitchen.

Nothing appealed to her. In fact, most foods made her stomach turn. She thought crackers might be the only food she could keep down. She grabbed a box from the cupboard and a bottle of club soda. She hated ginger ale.

She didn't want to sit at the table, she hated sitting in the kitchen. The couch looked so inviting. Crackers in one hand and soda in the other, she went to the living room. She grabbed the remote, turned on the food channel, and nibbled on the crackers. Her headache was almost gone, no more spots swimming in front of her eyes, and her stomach had settled. The crackers and soda worked. She felt better.

Tonight she would just relax and go to sleep early. She needed to be at work tomorrow. This debacle with the exhibit coming in months early had the entire department scrambling. The museum security had been under pressure to ensure the artifacts' safety— and tempers were short.

Her home phone rang, not her cell. Only her mother and grandmother called that number.

"Mom, hi... I'm fine, honest... I'm sitting here relaxing... You don't need to come over... I'm going to bed early... Honest... I know you would... I love you, too. Goodbye."

She hung up the phone and cursed Meredith under her breath. Before she could finish her soda, the doorbell rang. Tayla made her way to the door. She peeked out the window. Dene stood there with his hands in his pockets, rocking back and forth.

Dene had on ripped jeans and a tight polo. He looked hot. Breathtaking. Dene paced, and looked very nervous.

"For the love of..." She wasn't dressed for company. She grabbed the afghan and wrapped it around her.

Her heart pounded and her hands started to shake. She could barely contain her excitement. Anxiousness and desire coursed through her veins.

She ran her fingers through her hair and opened the door.

"Good evening, Tayla."

"Dene, why are you here?"

"I — I thought I would come by and make sure you are feeling better."

She stepped to the side. "Please, come in." Tayla couldn't take her eyes off him. Her heart felt like it was beating a thousand times a minute. She hoped he didn't notice how nervous being this close to him made her. "Can I get you anything?" Her voice squeaked as she asked, and she could feel her face flush. She couldn't keep still.

"I came here to check on you. It is I who should be asking you that question."

She watched as he paced the floor with his hands jammed in his pockets. The moon shone in through the window and washed over Dene, added a luminescence to his skin that made him even more good looking.

She felt her face grow hot. "Where are my manners? Please, sit down."

Dene crossed the room in two strides, his long muscular legs straining under his jeans, and Tayla was transfixed by his movement. She continued to watch him, mentally undressing him while thinking of all the ways she wanted him. Thoughts of their kiss taunted and emboldened her. His cologne tickled her nose and aroused her. She inhaled deeply, her eyes never leaving his. She shivered despite the heat of the room.

Dene moved closer and took her hand in his, the roughness of his hand gently enveloping hers. "I am sorry you did not feel well today. If there is anything I can do to help you feel better, it would be my pleasure."

Tayla gazed at his face then dropped her eyes, letting them trace a path down his physique. Her eyes fluttered to a brief stop on the solid ridges of his chest, noticing the faint outline of his nipples beneath his shirt. The degree of her arousal made her flush with heat and a touch of embarrassment. Her eyes continued their exploration of his body, dropping from his chest to his solid abs, then taking in the tight-fitting jeans that accentuated the long hard muscles of his thighs.

She licked her lips and found her gaze drifting to his midsection. The mental imagery flashing through her head was so wicked that she couldn't contain herself. Tayla reached for Dene, her hands encircling his waist with such suddenness that he stopped breathing for a moment.

"Tayla," he whispered breathlessly.

She moved one hand from his waist to softly touch his mouth, then traced his lips with her fingertips, and he involuntarily sucked in a deep breath. Tayla nibbled on his ear lobes then kissed his neck, relishing the feeling of his body reacting to her.

"Not here," she whispered. She took his hand and led him into her bedroom. As she closed the door, she turned and dropped the afghan she still had wrapped around her. She stood facing him in her silk peignoir.

"You're beautiful," Dene hoarsely whispered, lust drying his mouth.

For a moment, Tayla just drank in the vision of Dene, but then a smile flitted briefly across her lips. She moved closer to him and shyly traced the muscles of his arm with her fingertips. She impatiently moved both hands to his waistband then grabbed his shirt and tugged it off. Dene's breathing quickened.

Tayla caressed his muscular chest and a groan escaped his lips. She softly echoed the sound, enjoying the feel of his strength beneath her hand. She teased him by nibbling her way down his neck and kissing across his bare chest, pausing only slightly to work at unbuttoning his jeans.

Dene twitched beneath her soft caresses. In response, Tayla grasped the tab of his zipper and slowly pulled it down, one tooth at time, exposing Dene's boxers little by little. He reached to help her, but she stopped him. She was in control of this. Tayla brushed the back of her hand against his confined hardness then finished unzipping his pants. She slid her hands inside his waistband and teasingly began removing his jeans.

Leaning in, she brushed her lips against his belly, trailing kisses downward to the silken plane of his lower abs, pulling his boxers down around his thighs and out of the way. Dene's body responded, his length jumping in anticipation as she kissed her way closer and closer to his shaft and he pulled her to him. Tayla leaned back out of his reach, shaking her head—she wanted this to be on her terms. She licked up the length of his shaft, twirled her tongue around the tip of him, then took him into her mouth, gliding sensuously over the silky hard flesh. Dene breathed out in a rush while Tayla wandered so intimately around his genitals. She ran her hand across his thighs, eliciting a moan from Dene and felt him involuntarily twitching in her mouth. She alternately licked and sucked him, leisurely pleasuring him without trying to bring him to orgasm. Listening to his moans of pleasure and knowing she was causing them made Tayla wet.

As satisfying and provocative as her actions were, Tayla required more. She wanted to caress every inch of his body. With one last erotic swirl, Tayla popped Dene from her mouth and stood to meet his lips. Violently crushing her lips against his, she kissed him with open-mouthed passion, their tongues frenziedly dancing.

Dene moved his hand up to Tayla's breast, cupping it in one swift motion and stroking the nipple with his thumb. She leaned into his hand, enjoying the manipulation, and let him slide the strap of her baby-doll down her arm. She shrugged off the other strap and let the silky wrap puddle around her feet. She felt like a goddess standing against him in just her thong, her nipples hard and her body flushed with desire.

Dene rolled her against him so her back was to his chest, his shaft nestled between her buttocks, and made an inarticulate growl as he slid a hand into the front her thong. She moaned as he ran his fingers along her midline. With his other hand against her jaw, he bent her head back toward him until they could kiss, then he ran his hand back down to her breast, kneading the firm flesh and pinching the nipple.

His right fingers found her wet spot, and he slid them inside, rubbing her until she moaned and squirmed beneath him. He gently brushed against her clit, and Tayla pushed harder against his hand, making soft needy sounds. He stroked her until her wild gyrations had them both on the edge of no return. He broke their passion-filled kiss long enough to help her get her thong off quickly.

"Please," she begged, her voice husky," I need you inside me."

Tayla reached for him, her hand sliding over him, slick, hot. She drove him toward the bed and pushed him to his back, his shins and feet over the edge but still touching the floor.

"Please don't stop." He groaned, his manhood straining against her hand.

She leaned down, trailed her tongue over his lower abs, then licked his belly as she straddled his thighs. She continued her kissing-and-licking trail up his body as she slowly crawled toward his head until her sex teased his shaft, but didn't allow any penetration. Slowly she moved her hips, rubbed him with her own wetness, and he writhed in pleasure beneath her.

"Please," he begged.

She kept exploring, every touch eliciting an equally gratifying response. She had him at her mercy

Tayla stared into his eyes and watched him as he put his hands behind his head. She posed over him and worked herself toward climax. She teased him — delighted that she aroused him. He caressed her breasts, and she looked down at his hands, wrapped her own hands over his, encouraging him to squeeze her harder. She moaned, her sheath beginning to tighten around him. A flush signaling the nearing orgasm started working up her breasts toward her face.

Tayla relinquished control to him. He slid his hands from Tayla's breasts to her back and pulled her down onto him, then he cupped her ass as he continued to piston into her. Pressing her to him, he quickly rolled her onto her back, came up off her chest, and pulled her higher to him. She squirmed and started to buck against him. Their combined breaths came faster, and his jackhammer pumping had Tayla seeing stars. She squeezed her thighs tighter around his hips, keeping up with his furious pounding, and when he brought his thumb down to her clit she started a short staccato of sharp cries.

She panted and her body shook violently, each word spaced by a breath "Ahhh, Dene, I…"

"Finish," he growled, slamming into her again and again. Tayla clenched around him.

"Tayla, please," Dene gasped.

She arched her back, pushed her hips hard against him and cried out. "Dene!" Tayla's eyes widened and she wailed. She threw her head back in ecstasy, her nipples hardening to a point just shy of pain. Dene followed not a second behind.

They lay there for a minute basking in the sheer, exhausted contentment of the moment, then helped each other disentangle. They lay down snuggled against one another, kissing softly and coming back down to earth within each other's arms, blanket securing them.

"That was—"

#

Someone banged on the front door.

Tayla slid out of Dene's arms and pulled on a t-shirt and shorts. "Stay here. I'll be right back."

She made her way to the door and peered out. A curse escaped her lips. "Bennett, what are you doing here?"

"I saw Meredith. She told me you had a migraine and didn't go to work. I'm here to check on you. Aren't you going to let me in?"

"Bennett, let's not do this now."

"Do what?"

"I need some space. Time to think. I'm not sure it's going to work out between us."

"Tayla, baby. Let me in. Let's talk."

"Not tonight. We'll talk later."

"I'm not leaving. I'm going to stay right here until you let me in."

The banging continued. Tayla sighed and opened the door. "Two minutes." She stepped aside, just enough to let him into the foyer, but blocked the entrance to the living room.

"Let's sit, we'll be more comfortable." Bennett took her hand and led them to the couch. He slid his hand around her shoulder.

Tayla removed his arm, stood, and walked to the chair across the room. "I'm not ready for this. I told you. I think you should leave."

"Someone's here?"

"What?"

"I see the glasses. Where is he?"

"He who?"

Bennett stood and faced her. "So, you asked me for time to think, but have already moved on to someone else. That's great. I'm concerned about your health, drop what I'm doing to see you, and you've got a date."

"What I do is none of your business. I told you I need time."

"If you need time, then why are there two glasses?"

"You need to leave. Now."

Bennett stood and turned to face her. "This isn't over. You're mine. We're perfect together." Then he pushed past her and went down the hall toward the bedrooms.

"Stop. Right. There."

"Hiding someone?" He flung open her bedroom door.

Tayla followed him inside her room, body trembling. A sigh of relief escaped her lips. Dene had hidden or gone somewhere. She grabbed her phone from the nightstand.

"You need to leave before I call the police. Don't come back. We're through."

"Don't be ridiculous. This is all a misunderstanding. I love you. We're perfect for each other."

"Leave."

"You'll regret this. I'm the best thing that ever happened to you. Just wait. Tomorrow you'll be begging for me to take you back."

"We're finished. It hasn't been good between us for a long time. You don't appreciate me. I'm just something for you to own." She stomped over to the door and opened it. "Get out, and don't come back."

CHAPTER TWELVE

What just happened? Did they really make love? What was he thinking? She had a boyfriend. He wouldn't be the one to ruin her relationship. He would keep his distance. Be professional.

The night air cleared his head. The walk helped him regain his focus. He needed to teach Zet his next lesson and continue looking for MerNeith. That would be the only way this insufferable curse would be broken. He quickened his pace.

Thank the gods her boyfriend came in when he did. He may have lain with her again. She intrigued him. He could feel the draw, the attraction. Physically, she looked nothing like his lover, but sexually, she knew his desires. Her touch made him feel alive. Could she be his true love? Perhaps he was not meant to have the queen, but to be happy with someone else. Maybe that is the lesson his gods were trying to teach him. But—

He could not get Tayla out of his mind. Her soft skin, her gentle touch. The way she aroused him. Could he be happy with another? Thoughts of her clouded his mind, and before long, he had reached his living quarters.

Shalhoub was sitting at the table when he walked in. His face pale.

"Good evening, Siamun."

He looked up, but said nothing.

"Is something wrong?"

"He... Zet... Knife... Dead..."

"I don't understand. What are you trying to tell me?"

"The police detective. He, he questioned me about the dead security guard. I lied to him."

Not like he could tell the detective the truth, no one would believe him. "Do not worry. You are safe. He will not harm you. He needs you."

"And when he doesn't?"

"I will protect you."

"Great. A servant protecting me. From his pharaoh. I don't stand a chance."

Dene could feel his face getting hot. "I am not his servant. I am his advisor. I am bound by the curse. I must help him learn what he needs to pass each god's test. Then I shall be free of him."

"The detective will be back. He knows something."

"How could he know anything? I am sure you did not say anything."

"Of course not. But he said he would be coming to the museum tomorrow. He wants to question Tayla. And he said he may have more questions for everyone else. "

The detective was not his problem. He had been lying and stealing for centuries to protect himself and Zet. He could handle one law official. The bigger problem was Tayla. His feelings for her. How could he contain them as he searched for MerNeith and taught Zet his new lesson?

A vision of Meredith swam before his eyes. She looked like MerNeith, had the same tattoo, but... Something about her nagged at him. The attraction just wasn't there. In his time, he could not keep from thinking about her. Now, she was like a friend. And if he thought hard about it, she was not interested in him, either. He could tell she liked him as a friend, she made that clear, and some days she even flirted, but it was all in fun. He needed to continue his search

He turned to Shalhoub again. "Have you seen Zet? I must continue his lessons. He was supposed to be here."

"I'm glad he isn't. I don't trust him. If you knew what was good for you, you would distance yourself from him."

"Would that it were that simple. As I have explained to you, we are tied together by this insufferable curse."

"Is there no other way? Some spell or something?"

"There is no spell. I am bound. Know this, I may have to help him move on, but I do not need to make his life happy."

The door opened and the pharaoh strolled in. "I'm ready for my lesson. Come on. Teach me. I do not have all evening. My queen is out there, waiting for me."

Dene turned toward him and pointed to the table. Shalhoub tugged at his collar. Zet pulled out a chair across from him.

"Leave. We do not need your presence."

Shalhoub crossed his arms. "I'll be leaving when I am finished. Don't worry, I won't interfere with your lesson."

Zet rose and crossed to Shalhoub. "Do not make me ask again. I will not tolerate your disrespect."

Shalhoub stood and faced him. "Don't threaten me. You need me. I got rid of the body from the museum. The man you killed. I gave you a place to stay, gave you money, helped you with the museum staff."

Dene stepped in between them. "He may stay if he wishes. Perhaps he can help us in our search for the sec—"

"I'm done helping him." Shalhoub turned and stormed out the door.

#

The night went by slowly. Zet did not pay attention. Dene's patience wore thin. "You will never be free from the curse if you do not take it seriously. Now let us get back to work."

"I have done all you have asked of me tonight. I am done for the evening. We will continue this tomorrow." He stood and headed to the door.

Dene stepped in front of him. "I am cursed to help you learn your lessons. I have spent the last four thousand years with you. From solstice to solstice every one hundred years."

Zet waved his hand in front of Dene's face. "What is the point of your complaint? I have learned every lesson that you have taught me. I have passed each of the god's tests. We will be free of the curse this time, I feel it."

"We have very little time. I need you to take this seriously."

The king fluffed him off with a wave of his hand. "You have nothing to worry about. I will learn this lesson and pass the god's test."

"Do you truly believe that the gods are fooled by you? You have passed their tests simply because you knew their secret names. But unless you actually learn your lesson and become a good, kind, decent person, you will not pass the weighing of the heart."

"Silence." He pointed his finger in Dene's face. "I will pass. And if I do not, it will be because you did not do your part."

"If you do not change your attitude, you will not pass. You will be the first pharaoh ever to fail to get to the afterlife. And I do not wish to be damned for all eternity."

Zet's phone rang. "I'm leaving. I will return later."

#

Dene could feel his face getting hotter. Even the cool breeze that came in the door Zet left open did nothing to cool him down. Zet would never learn his lesson. He would curse them for eternity. His only hope would be to find the queen and have her fall in love with him.

His mind drifted to the earlier evening with Tayla. Her floral perfume, her soft skin, like a beacon calling to him. Her gentle touch made him insane. If only she did not have a boyfriend, he felt he could be very happy with her. She deserved better than him, though. If he could not break the curse and she fell in love with him, when the solstice came he would be gone, and she would be alone.

Another life ruined because of Zet. No, he would not pursue her. He needed to concentrate on finding his queen and teaching Zet his lessons.

His phone rang. The caller ID showed Tayla's name. He decided not to answer, he would see her tomorrow. Tayla rang again, so he ignored the call. Her voice rang in his head. He closed his eyes and relived making love to her. That too-recent memory began to arouse him again. He shook his head. A cold shower should work. He needed to get her out of his mind for all of the reasons he kept thinking about. The ice cold water did nothing to help him.

Michele Jones

CHAPTER THIRTEEN

Zet appeared in a huff. "Dene, I have been waiting for you for more than five clock ticks. You were to be here to start my lesson."

"I am here. Something came up."

"I do not care about your problems. We need to focus on me. Now, let us start the lesson."

"As you wish."

The king and Dene worked on the lesson for hours.

"I tire of this. I believe that I know enough to pass this test. Let us go and enjoy the day."

"You do not understand the lesson. You must practice. If you do not pass, the curse will continue and neither of us will go on to the afterlife."

"Of course I will pass. I know what I need to do."

"Your heart must be lighter than the feather. Do you honestly think that the gods will believe your false statements? That you have changed your ways? We watched you kill the security guard."

"He was not important, nor did we need his services. I do not believe that he will keep me from passing. But if you must know, I do not believe that I will need to pass the test. I have found my queen. I will be granted a human life here, where I will have a whole other lifetime to learn these infernal lessons."

The two argued for several minutes. Dene kept trying to teach the lesson that Zet needed to learn, but he was not focused on learning. After several attempts, Zet ended the lesson and vanished, leaving Dene standing there.

CHAPTER FOURTEEN

Tayla picked up her cell and texted Meredith.

Come over for some wine?

The reply was instantaneous.

I'm on my way.

Tayla poured a glass of white wine and walked to the living room. She set it on the coffee table and paced. How did things get this out of control? Her argument with Bennett allowed Dene to get away. But her relationship with Bennett was over. In her heart she knew that even before they went out for their anniversary. Things had been strained. She had hoped that they would be able to work out their problems, and that their anniversary date would save the relationship, but it made her realize it wasn't going to work.

She grabbed a bag from the kitchen and walked around taking down pictures of Bennett. Each one she grabbed dug a deeper hole in her heart. The one on the end table, taken at Kennywood, their first official date. She took down the picture on the mantle that was taken at Meredith's "Because I Wanted To" barbecue. She loved that picture. They looked so perfect. They had been together for almost two years.

After a deep breath, she continued. More pictures needed to be taken down. She took down the framed ones from the hall as she made her way to the bedroom. She looked around and pictures of Bennett littered the room—the nightstand, dresser, chest of drawers, the walls. How had they come to this?

Last, Tayla went to her office. On her desk she had a picture of Bennett playing Scrabble. He was so competitive. It was noticeable in the look of concentration on his face. She opened the bottom drawer of her filing cabinet. Inside there were photo albums, filled with happier times. Memories she shared with Bennett, her family, and her friends. She went through the albums, removing the photos of Bennett. A tear trickled down her face.

He had been part of her life for more than five years. Now, that was all behind her. Even though they were not together anymore, she didn't want to throw the pictures away. She tucked the bag in the back of her entry closet. Someday, maybe they would be friends. But she wasn't ready for that just yet.

#

Meredith came through the door and called out, "Tayla, where are you?"

"I'll be right out."

When Tayla came out, Meredith was sitting on the chair, leg over the side, hair pulled back, dressed in leggings and a beater.

"Thought you might like to go for a run."

"I asked you over for drinks."

"I know what you asked, but it's not what you need. I see you did some house cleaning."

Tayla slumped onto the couch and put her head in her hands. The tears flowed and the sobbing went on for several minutes. She felt Meredith's hand go around her shoulders and pull her close. Her best friend always knew what she needed. After what seemed to be an eternity she lifted her head. "Thanks for letting me get that out."

"That's what friends are for. Now tell me everything."

Where to start? There was so much to tell. Should she start with the breakup? Or her attraction to Dene? She knew Meredith wouldn't judge, but sleeping with Dene? Was that something she wanted to confess?

Tayla stood and headed to the kitchen. "I need something to drink. I have a Zinfandel chilling in the fridge. What would you like?"

"I'm not interested in the wine. Tell me what happened."

Damn, she got straight to the point. Tayla hadn't invited her here for wine and chocolates. She needed to talk to someone. She needed confirmation from her best friend that she did the right thing. And she knew that Meredith would tell it like it was.

"It's a long story."

"I have all night."

It definitely was going to be a long night. Tayla stood and paced the living room. "It's over."

"Hallelujah. It's about time you ditched that loser."

"You used to like him—"

"I did. But that was before you started having issues. And crying. The last straw was seeing him out with another woman. Especially when I knew he was supposed to be with you."

"Well, that's all behind us now. I told him we needed to take a break. That I needed time to think things out."

"Tay, you need to move on. You haven't been happy with him for the longest time."

"It's not that easy. He was a big part of my life for more than five years. We have a history."

"And crying for the last couple months has been the biggest part of that history."

Meredith crossed the room, sat on the couch by Tayla, and put her arm around her shoulders. "It will get better. Promise."

"I know, I—"

The phone interrupted her. Meredith reached across the table and grabbed it before Tayla could get it. She answered it, but didn't say anything further. After a few seconds, she hung up.

"Who—"

"Nobody was there."

"It was Bennett, wasn't it?"

"Honestly, Tay, nobody was on the other end. And the caller ID was private."

Tayla started crying and shook uncontrollably. "I honestly didn't think this would affect me the way it has. I know we weren't getting along. And we were fighting all the time. But it still hurts."

Meredith grabbed Tayla's hands, assuring her it would get better. Truth be told, Tayla was more upset that she had let it get to this point than she was with the breakup. She knew she would be okay, she didn't need Meredith for that. She just needed someone to listen to her, to be understanding. Meredith told her she thought she should end it long ago. She saw things going down the wrong path. But did she listen? No. She had to try. She thought it was her fault. Turns out, Meredith was right all along. And she would let her know. Not tonight, but she would let her know.

Tayla grabbed a Kleenex and wiped her face. She stood up, pushed her hair back from her face, and headed to the kitchen. She grabbed the wine, a couple of glasses, the electric bottle opener, potato chips, and the M&Ms. Chocolate and wine go together. Right? And she had chips as a backup plan, just in case.

She wandered back from the kitchen and set everything down on the coffee table. After opening the wine, she poured two glasses and then opened the M&Ms. She sorted them as she held her wine, mindlessly eating the brown ones first. Meredith grabbed the chips, opened the bag, and munched on them. She pushed her wine to the side.

"Told you we needed wine."

"You're not drinking your wine. You're just holding it, and you're stalling."

Tayla stood and paced the room.

"I'm here for you. Talk to me." Meredith stood and faced her. "I know you're hurting, but seriously, you know it was for the best. You'll be much happier."

Tayla wiped the tears again. "I know. I just wish it were easier."

"It will be. You need something to take your mind off things. Let's go for a run, or to the gym."

"I'm really not in the mood." She was now eating the orange M&Ms.

"C'mon. Trust me. You'll feel better."

She needed to get out of her house. Too many memories. The run should clear her head. And it was a nice night. "I'll change. Give me a minute." She grabbed all the yellow M&Ms. It took her less than five minutes to get ready. She pulled her hair back into a ponytail and grabbed two waters from the fridge. "Ready."

They ran in silence for almost an hour. Through the neighborhood, down past their old school, then back through the neighborhood, before finishing at the diner down the street from her house. Meredith was right. The run did help. Her muscles protested, but it was a great feeling. Her mind was finally clear and she was ready to move on. Truthfully, she had been ready to move on months ago. She just kept hoping for things to change. There was one last time she needed to see Bennett—to return his ring. Meredith could help her pack his things, and she would call him to get them at the end of the week.

Meredith pulled the door to the diner. "Let's get a drink and a pizza. Then we'll go back to your house, and I'll help you get rid of all things Bennett."

The girls went inside and sat at a booth far from the bar. They ordered pizza and beer and talked about Bennett. It felt good to get everything off her chest. Especially the part about Bennett saying she would regret it, and that she would beg him to take her back.

"I thought he was the one. But after I met Dene, I've been having second thoughts."

Tayla continued the Dene conversation with Meredith. She couldn't explain it, but something about him really drew her to him. He was mysterious, but not really. The way he spoke. His English was good, but he didn't know American slang. And those turquoise eyes. They sparkled when he spoke. His passion for his country, and his love of its history. It drew her to him, and it didn't hurt that he was built.

"Are you sure that you aren't using him as a rebound guy?"

"It's not like that. He's easy to be around. I feel connected to him."

"Tay, don't you think you're moving a bit too fast? You just dumped Bennett."

"No. I can't explain it, but there's something there." Tayla took a breath and whispered, "and I slept with him."

"You what?"

"You heard that? Please don't say anything. I don't want anyone to know. I'm not sure where this is going."

"Details."

"Dene came over to see how I was feeling. I invited him in, and we sat together on the couch. I wanted him. I can't explain it, but I was drawn to him. He held my hand. One thing led to another and we started kissing and touching each other. It was so sensual and intense. We made our way to the bedroom—Well, you can fill in the rest."

#

Bennett wasn't done with Tayla. He went to the store, got what he needed, parked outside her house, and waited. She would call Meredith, and Meredith would come running over. Then they would go out. Tayla did this all the time. Meredith was Tayla's security blanket, her confidant.

Ah, how well he knew her. Within the half hour, Meredith showed up. Break up with him, would she? He'd teach her. He was the best thing that ever happened to her.

He had a plan. Roses. Tayla hated roses, and that was the flower he chose. First, he left a bouquet on her front porch. She wouldn't know it was him.

He had a key, but that would be too obvious. He used a crowbar to pry open the door and let himself inside. He had told her to get an alarm, but of course she hadn't listened. Now, he would break in and no one would know until she came home. Three glasses of wine on the table, plus M&Ms and chips. She was upset, the M&Ms told him that. But the extra glass? Who was she entertaining?

He needed to make it look like a break-in. He tore apart her house, overturning drawers, taking things out of her closet, and trashing her kitchen. He pulled out his knife and cut her couch, throwing the stuffing around and destroying the rest of the pieces. Then he trailed rose petals throughout her house, throwing the stems on the floor. He left another large arrangement on the mantle, where a photo of them used to be, then made his way to her bedroom. The bed was unmade. Did the mystery wine drinker share her bed? She would pay for that.

Bennett went to her nightstand and took out a lace nightie, ripped it, and laid it carefully in the center of the bed. He tore apart a rose, left the stem on her pillow, and threw the petals on her bed. He pulled out his knife and shredded the other pillow. Then he opened her drawers and rooted though her closet.

She needed to know someone was there. She needed to be afraid. He went into the master bathroom and drew a bubble bath. He floated rose petals on the surface, leaving the stems on the floor. Finally, after lighting a few candles, he left.

Tayla would have to call him. She wouldn't know what to do, and she would be afraid. This break-in would make her realize she needed him.

Bennett looked around one last time, left her front door wide open, and then went and hid across the street. He needed to see the fear on her face when she came home.

He didn't need to wait long. Not even ten minutes later, he saw Tayla and Meredith walking toward her house. When she saw her house had been broken into, she would be so afraid, she would call him to come over. He pulled his phone out of his pocket, put it on vibrate, and waited for her call.

It never came. Neither Tayla nor Meredith called him. But they called someone. His nostrils flared and he clenched his fists as he saw Tayla on her phone. Was she calling the man that she shared the glass of wine with?

Tayla belonged to him. He would never let her be with another man. Never.

Michele Jones

CHAPTER FIFTEEN

The police told her to wait until they got there before going inside her house. She had no intention of going inside. Whoever broke in could still be there. Doubtful, but she wasn't betting her life on it. Tayla paced the street, Meredith alongside her. Where were the police? How long did it take? They could be dead before the police arrived. She needed to call her parents. They needed to know, and it would be better coming from her than from a concerned neighbor.

Tayla trembled thinking about someone breaking into her home. This was a quiet neighborhood. Things like this didn't happen there. Why her? She certainly didn't have the biggest house on the block. Never bothered anyone. Participated in the neighborhood activities. Unbelievable.

Two police cars pulled in front of Tayla's house, the cops exited and approached the girls. "Ms. Amari?"

"I'm Tayla Amari."

"Did you enter the house?"

Tayla responded, "No, sir. We were instructed not to."

The officers drew their guns. "Wait here."

Tayla and Meredith stepped back and waited as the officers checked out the house. Minutes later they were back and gave the all clear to enter.

"Clear." The officer turned toward the girls. "Ms. Amari, follow us. We need to know if anything is missing."

Tayla and Meredith followed the officers. Tayla paused at the flowers by her door. She hesitated, breathing fast, before continuing on.

"Ms. Amari, would—"

"Oh. My. God." Tayla shot her hands out, using the door jamb to catch herself. Inside, everything had been destroyed. Furniture ruined. Flower petals and stems everywhere. Wine glasses broken. Her stomach clenched. On the mantle, a pristine vase filled with roses.

"Ms. Amari? We need you to tell us if anything is missing."

Tayla crossed her arms across her chest. "I—I don't know."

Noise came from the porch. Tayla could hear gruff muffled voices, but couldn't decipher the words. Someone wanted in. Seconds later, Detective Flanagan entered.

#

Bennett fumed. He saw everything. Tayla made another call. Who to this time? Why hadn't she called him? This wasn't over by any means. He needed to make her realize she needed him.

The bushes provided him perfect cover. But he was losing his patience with her. She made another call, again not to him. What's wrong with her? Didn't she realize she needed him? What would make her come back to him? Next time, he would use his key. He'd install cameras. Maybe find out who the mystery man was. Make subtle changes. Eventually she'll call. She needed him. And if he couldn't have her, well—

He dialed her number but didn't hit send. He almost made a fatal mistake. He almost called her from his phone. She needed to be afraid. She had to realize she needed him. He dug the burner phone out of his back pocket. Blocked the number. He could call her whenever, and nobody would know it was him. A smug smile crossed his lips. He punched in her number and hit send.

He couldn't see her in the house, but that didn't bother him. All he needed was to hear her the fear in her voice. First call. He hung up after two rings. Second call. Voice mail. Third call. "Hello?"

His body pulsed with excitement.

"Hello?"

Silence.

"Who is this?"

Dead air. He started breathing harder into the phone, then ended the call.

Bennett watched the police exit Tayla's house and start going through the neighborhood. He shoved everything into his pockets and walked through the yard to his car. They wouldn't find him. He'd be long gone.

#

Tayla slumped to the floor. She couldn't take much more. First she ended her relationship Bennett. Next her house gets broken into. And now someone was calling her cell phone and not talking.

The officers pressed for her to continue through the house.

"Ms. Amari, we need to know if anything is missing. But don't touch anything. Once you've gone through and looked around, we'll dust for prints."

Tayla and Meredith continued through the house looking at the damage. How could she possibly know if something was missing? Everything had been ruined. Meredith steadied her as they walked through the kitchen. Broken glasses, wine bottle smashed on the floor, doors torn off their hinges. How would she ever feel safe here?

Only a few rooms remained.

They stood in the doorway to her bedroom. Tayla clenched her stomach. Tears ran down her cheeks. Who could possibly hate her this much? She turned and ran down the hall and into the living room. She had to get out of there. Immediately. In her haste, she ran into someone taking notes.

"I'm sorry," she mumbled.

"No problem." he said.

He turned toward her. "Ms. Amari. I'd like to ask you a few questions."

"Detective, why are you here? This is just a break in."

"The officers called me. They believe there's more to this."

"Are you kidding me? This can't be happening."

"Detective Flanagan?"

He turned toward Meredith. "Ms. Nazari." His voice was softer, and his hard features lightened.

"Do you think this has something to do with Stan's murder?"

"I'd like you to come down to the station with me. My car's right outside." He turned to the officers. "Finish processing the scene. We'll talk later."

Tayla and Meredith grabbed their purses and went outside.

The detective walked over to his car and opened the doors. "Please, come with me."

"I'll drive. Besides, I need my car."

"I'd prefer you if you rode with me. Just as a precaution."

What precaution? What did he know? Did he think whoever did this was still around with all the police here? Tayla couldn't believe all that had happened in such a short time. Her house wasn't safe anymore. Not until they caught whoever had done this. And now she had to be driven to the police station. Under guard. "Very well."

The all got into the detective's car and went to the station. This would be a long night.

#

Dene could not get Tayla out of his mind. She consumed his every thought and invaded his dreams. His time was short, and he needed to focus on teaching Zet his next lesson. Another exercise in futility. Zet did not want to learn his lessons, he just wanted to learn what he needed to get past the god's tests. The king was so naive. He believed he could trick the gods. But Dene knew better. Zet would only fail the test, and doom them both for all eternity. Neither would get to the afterlife. Even Zet could not find the secret names of the gods. They only had one other chance. Find the queen reincarnate.

Zet believed that he had found his queen. Meredith. And he made his plans based on that assumption. Dene did not understand. Even though she looked like MerNeith, the attraction simply wasn't there. He felt nothing, not even a slight draw.

To his dismay, he connected with Tayla. Emerald eyes, olive skin, long legs. Nothing like the queen. And she could not help him pass to the afterlife. She could not even help him live out a mortal life. The only thing he could give to her would be misery.

In a few short months, he would be gone, and if he continued to pursue her, she would be hurt. His abilities were already fading. It had become more difficult to transport. She deserved better. But he wanted her.

The night he spent with her, before they were interrupted, he felt something he had not experienced in ages. His body responded to her. He grew hard just thinking of her. Dene unbuttoned his jeans and unzipped the fly. Thoughts of Tayla consumed him and his erection grew harder. Sliding his hand into his boxers, he quickly stroked himself a few times. The feeling of his rough hand on his sensitive flesh was no help—it merely inflamed his desires. He paced to the bathroom and turned on the shower then tore off his shirt and his jeans as fast as he could.

His palms started sweating with anxiety even as his erection throbbed. He dove under the cold, pulsing shower head, hoping for salvation, but it did nothing. He was harder than before, and he ached to bury himself in Tayla. He closed his eyes and remembered her face in the throes of ecstasy—as he'd seen his queen so many centuries ago. Taking the soap in his hands, he lathered them then turned his back to the cold water. He reached down and began stroking himself with an unrelenting rhythm. Every stroke dragged a tortured moan from Dene.

Tayla, please, do not make me beg.

Cold water sluiced down over his body but still no relief. He reached out to lean one hand on the shower stall, but then put his left shoulder against the wall instead, while his right hand continued at a furious pace.

Praise the gods, please help me.

He reached down with his left hand and squeezed his scrotum. The pleasure of his right hand mixed with the pinching tightness of his left hand was just enough to bring his mind closer to allowing release. Dene's thighs shook and he clenched his ass with each stroke, thrusting into his hand as he would into his beloved. He gripped himself tighter with both hands but moved his right hand faster. His body reacted to his touch and he moaned. Releasing his shaft, he balled his fist against the shower wall, pounded it in rhythm with the pummeling water. He arched his back, water cascading over his taut muscles, and he violently came. His body shuddered with each continued follow up stroke. Finally finished, he slumped against the shower wall, letting the cold water continue to weep shameful rivulets down his back.

#

Dene toweled off, exhausted from moments before. These past days affected him in ways he could not comprehend. He wrapped a towel around his waist and went to the living room.

"This isn't ancient Egypt," Shalhoub said. "For God's sake, put some clothes on."

"This is infinitely more comfortable than modern day restrictive clothing. Perhaps you should try it."

"We aren't doing this. I was forced to help you, but I didn't agree to this."

Dene didn't move. "My only desire is to be comfortable." Why must everything be so difficult?

"While making me uncomfortable."

A loud banging at the door interrupted them. Dene stood and headed toward his bedroom. "I shall change as you answer the door."

"Detective Flanagan. I thought you were interviewing all of us at the office tomorrow." Dene heard Shalhoub as he finished changing.

"This isn't a social call. May I come in?"

Dene made his way to the living room. "Detective. I trust you are well? How can we help you?"

The detective dove straight in. "Where were each of you this evening? And where is Zet?"

Dene communicated to Zet telling him to return and come out of his room.

"We've been here all evening. Is something wrong at the museum? Is there a problem with the exhibit?"

"I'm not here about the exhibit. Ms. Amari's house was broken into—"

Dene asked, "Is Tay—Ms. Amari all right? Tell me. What happened?"

"I'm the one asking the questions."

"Forgive me. I am simply concerned for Ms. Amari's safety. Please. Tell me. Is she okay?"

Zet strolled from his bedroom, pushed passed the detective, and sat on the couch. Dene shook his head in disbelief. Arms crossed, he turned to Zet and filled him in communicating silently.

"Ms. Amari is fine. This is the second incident connected to the museum in days, and the department is investigating everyone."

Dene offered the detective a seat. He continued to stand. After several more questions, the detective called it a night. "I'll see everyone in the morning."

CHAPTER SIXTEEN

Tayla appreciated Meredith letting her crash with her. She couldn't stay at her place, because it was still a crime scene. Even when they released it, it would be days before she cleaned it up. If she cleaned it up. Tayla stared at the clock. Midnight. The weekend events kept her mind racing. She couldn't sleep. She went over the questions Detective Flanagan asked her. Why would the break-in at her house be related to Stan's death? She had nothing in common with Stan other than working at the museum. Stan's death. The mysterious rearrangement of the exhibit room. Her house break-in. How could they be connected?

A soft knock at the door. "You up? Want some company?" Meredith whispered.

Great. Now she was keeping her friend awake. "C'mon in. I couldn't sleep."

Meredith opened the door and plopped down on the bed. "Tay, it'll be okay." She put her arm around her friend's shoulders.

Tayla sighed. "I know. But I can't stop thinking about what could have happened if I had been at home. Did the intruder have a gun? Would he have tried to kill me?"

"Don't worry about that now. You weren't home and you're here. Safe. Nothing's going to happen to you. I won't let it."

"You can't be sure. If the detective is right, you could be next."

"You worry too much. I'm sure it was a random break in. Let's get some chamomile tea and try and get some rest. We have a long day ahead tomorrow."

Tayla knew Meredith was right. She gave into her imagination. Amazing how fear could change your perspective. She jumped off the bed and grabbed Meredith's hand. "Good idea. We both need our sleep."

#

The rest of the night passed uneventfully. The tea relaxed Tayla, but she remained awake. Stan's death, the break in, the rearranged museum exhibit. She couldn't connect them. How are they related? Think Tayla. What do all of these things have in common?

Stan. Museum. Break-in. Stan. Museum. Break-in.

She tried to connect them. Stan worked at the museum. The exhibit was in the museum. But the break-in at her house? How was that related?

The clock blinked 3:31 a.m. She had been working this puzzle for two hours. What tied everything together? The museum exhibit. Everything related to the museum. Stan, the rearranged exhibit. Even the break-in. She worked at the museum. That must be the connection. This couldn't wait. She had to tell Meredith. If she was right, Meredith could be next. She bolted out of bed and ran down the hall.

"Meredith. Meredith." She banged on Meredith's bedroom door. "Wake up. I've figured it out."

She heard Meredith groan. "Tayla, go back to bed. We'll talk in the morning."

"This can't wait. Get up." Tayla pictured her pulling the pillow over her head, trying desperately to go back to sleep. "Meredith, you need to get up. If I'm right, you're in danger."

The door opened, and Meredith swept her hand in across her body, gesturing her to come inside. "This better be good. We've got to be up for work in a few hours. And I can't function without a good eight hours."

"I know what everything has in common. Everything relates to the museum. Specifically, back to the exhibit."

"Stan? He had nothing to do with the exhibit."

"Wrong. He was the security guard on duty when the exhibit came in. And the rearranged exhibit room—"

"That nobody saw rearranged but you."

"As I was saying, the rearranged room. Part of the Egyptian exhibit."

"Seriously, I think you've lost it."

"What about your brother's accident? Coincidence? I think not."

"Your reaching at straws here. It was just an unfortunate accident."

Tayla continued on, not fazed by Meredith's lack of understanding. "And the break-in at my house. As part of the staff assigned to the Egyptian exhibit, I was targeted. Don't you see? It's right in front of our face. Someone is trying to scare us."

"Stan's murder? Part of a scare tactic? That's a bit extreme, don't you think? And why would someone want to scare us? That makes no sense at all."

"Ugh." Tayla paced the room. "Someone wants us to believe that we are subject to the curse. 'The Pharaoh's Curse.' All of those things are involved with an Egyptian pharaoh tomb."

"No, you are so far from the mark here."

"I don't think so. Someone wants us to think we are being cursed."

"What makes you think that?"

"A curse will be cast upon any person who disturbs the mummy of an Ancient Egyptian person, especially a pharaoh."

"You know that isn't true. Besides, we aren't grave robbers."

"Here me out. The curse doesn't differentiate between thieves and innocent people. The curse only refers to anyone who disturbs a mummy. And the curse isn't necessarily deadly. It can also cause bad luck or illness."

"That's a stretch. And you can't tell me that you believe in curses."

"Of course I don't. I'm saying someone is using the curse to get to us. Or they are trying to cover up something. Stan, the exhibit, my house. It all fits."

"Tay, even if you're right, what could they possibly be trying to cover up? And why kill Stan? Wouldn't hurting him work just as well?"

"Honestly, I don't know. But I'm telling you, that has to be the connection. That's the common denominator."

"If you're sure, then you need to tell Detective Flanagan. Maybe it will help him," Meredith replied.

#

Zet turned to Shalhoub. "Leave us. There are things that we must discuss."

Shalhoub threw his hands in the air. "I'll be in my room."

Zet turned toward Dene and communicated to him. *Shalhoub is insufferable. How dare he not listen to me.*

Dene responded. *He has helped you on numerous occasions. You are indebted to him.*

I may be indebted to him, but I do not need to listen to him or have him in my presence.

What did you want to speak with me regarding?

That detective. Why is he troubling us? He comes here with an accusatory tone. What would I possibly want with that girl? She's nothing to me.

He is simply doing his job. The detective is investigating the security guard that you killed, and then a break in at Tayla's house. He thinks they are related. He has no idea that you killed the guard.

And he never will. Besides, if you don't guide me better, we will not be here long enough to worry about it. I already feel myself fading. It takes me longer to materialize. So forget about that detective and concentrate on my next lesson. What am I to do to pass the next test?

Dene threw his hands in the air. Have you learned nothing? You need to be humble. Try being nice. A little kindness will go a long way. When the gods ask you the next set of questions, will your heart be pure? We both know the answer to that.

Don't take that tone with me.

I have spent the last four thousand years as your teacher. You have learned nothing. You do not follow my direction, and you have not passed the tests put before you.

You speak falsely. I passed several tests.

You feigned your way through them. Barely. Others, you were not even close.

It is your destiny to make sure I pass the tests. You are not holding up your end of the bargain.

Dene clenched his jaw. *Once a century I have an opportunity to teach you and help you get us both to the afterlife. Yet you do not take my instruction.*

You are not working hard enough.

I have worked tirelessly on your behalf. And I have saved us on many occasions. I cannot help with everything. You must take the time to learn. Anubis will not tolerate much more. He, Osiris, and Isis have been more than patient. You must be able to profess your innocence and purity. The way you behave, that will not be possible. There is only one tests left before the weighing of the heart. If you do not change your ways, you will doom us both for all eternity.

Dene left and returned with a book in his hand. He crossed the room and shoved the Book of the Dead into Zet's chest. *Read this. And learn from it. Perhaps there will be a clue as to the secret names of the gods in there. That's our only hope. Unless you have found our queen.*

Zet stormed across the room. *You are my servant. As such, you will do as I say, and not speak to me like an equal.*

Dene bowed his head and replied with a nod. *As you wish.* Then he dematerialized, leaving only a few grains of sand in his place.

#

Dene materialized close to Tayla's house. He stepped out from behind a tree and stared. Yellow tape blocked the entrance to her home.

CRIME SCENE DO NOT CROSS

Her house looked cold and empty. Almost lifeless. What happened? Thoughts of Tayla being attacked overtook him and made his hands shake. Did Zet try something? Was he responsible for this? Moments later, he was inside. What did he hope to find? He had no idea.

It took a moment for his eyes to adjust, but when they did, his stomach clenched. The living room had been destroyed. Furniture upended, broken glasses, and flowers strewn everywhere. Careful not to touch anything, he continued farther into her house.

Glass crunched beneath his feet as he tip-toed around the kitchen. It appeared to be worse than the living room. Cabinets open, broken dishes, an empty wine bottle on the floor, its contents scattered around it.

Did her intruder go into the bedroom? The room he shared with her the other night? Dene had to know. He carefully walked down the hall and peered in the open door. His heart sank, and his hands shook with rage.

The intruder entered her bedroom. Dene went inside, looked, and his jaw dropped. It wasn't the destroyed furniture, he had seen plenty of that. Clothes littered the floor, except for the torn lace nightie on the bed surrounded by flower petals and stems. He spun around and saw more flower petals and stems on the floor leading to the master bathroom.

He crept forward, threw the open door, and walked into her private bath chambers. What he saw sickened his stomach. More stems on the floor and flower petals floating in a drawn bath surrounded by candles.

Michele Jones

CHAPTER SEVENTEEN

Bennett's plan hadn't worked out exactly as he had planned. Tayla didn't call him. No matter, he had more planned for her. While at her house, he took her museum security pass and keys. Tayla was a creature of habit. Everything always in its place. Keys and security pass always in the left drawer of the console table in the foyer. The second drawer had the keys to her parents, his penthouse apartment, and Meredith's place. Those would come in handy later.

Break up with him? This would teach her. She was his girlfriend. She belonged to him. There was no way he would ever permit her to be with anyone else. They were the perfect couple. Everyone told him that. He wouldn't allow her to ruin his perfect image. She'd come back to him or—

A plan formed. Bennett remembered Tayla telling him about the curses associated with grave robbing an Egyptian tomb. That could be used to his advantage. Not only would he go after Tayla, but he would target the others associated with the exhibit. That would keep Tayla on edge.

The museum security card. That would gain him undetected entry into the museum, and if anyone checked, the only person who entered would be Tayla. He was so much smarter than she gave him credit for. This would make her call him for sure. He would be there to take her back, but he would make her beg just a little.

He put on torn jeans, a hoodie, dark glasses, the most beat up pair of boat shoes he owned, baseball cap, and headed out. Part two of his plan was to get her at work. But not just her — he needed to get the others as well.

The local stores wouldn't do, he had to go out of town. Somewhere he wouldn't be noticed. To ensure he wouldn't be noticed, he rented a car for a few days. The back road out of town was empty, he hadn't passed anyone in an hour. Perfect. The GPS guided him to his destination. Set for no highways, it took longer. Not a problem for him. He didn't want anyone to notice him. The first store was ahead on the right. Just one of the several stops planned before he went to the museum and redecorated her office.

Tayla would have to call him after this. She would be terrified and turn to him for comfort. He would take her back, of course, but he would make her beg. That would teach her to break up with him. She was his. They had been together for years, and if he couldn't have her, no one would.

Bennett kept his head down, purchased the flowers, and headed to his next stop. He didn't want to draw suspicion to himself. His plan called for him to get no more than two dozen roses at each store. One a.m. The trip for flowers lasted almost three hours.

Action. Backpack with flowers and note carefully slung over his shoulder. Car parked close, but out of sight. Bennett strode down the back streets and approached the employee entrance. The security camera focused on the door. After donning black gloves, he pulled the hood up, covering his head. Couldn't be too careful. He needed to get in unnoticed. Bennett took out the security card and the keys, kept his head down, and made his way to the door. After punching in her code—her grandfather's birthday—he entered the building and cautiously made his way to her office. Head down the entire time.

The offices had no security cameras. They were in a different wing than the exhibits. He wanted to get in, leave her the flowers and the note, and get out. Fifteen minutes should be enough time. He couldn't risk more than that. He pulled the key from his back pocket and let himself inside. Pitch black. The room had no windows. No external light. Bennett was prepared. He pulled out a small flashlight and went to work. Flower petals and stems strewn around the office, vase and note in the center of her desk.

It needed to look like a break-in. Had to seem like someone was targeting her as a victim of "the mummy's curse" so it didn't blow back on him. As quietly as he could, he trashed her office—turned out drawers, broke items on her desk, pulled things off her wall. That should do it.

He tiptoed to the door and switched off the flashlight. Cracked the door slightly and peered into the hall. Empty. Lowering his head, he made his way out of the building and to his car.

Fist pump. His body tingled. This should have her crawling back to him. He made it in and out without being seen. Now he had to return her keys. Shouldn't be a problem, the house was empty. Fifteen minutes later, he was in front of Tayla's house. He paused to make sure no one was there. No cars, no lights. The place looked deserted.

He pulled into a spot down the street. Staying hidden was paramount. Deciding the back door was the best place to enter, he jogged away from her house and turned the corner. Within minutes, he was inside. He crept along the wall, made his way to the foyer, and put the key and the security card back in the console table. If they checked the security log, it would be her ID that they saw. And she couldn't even say it had gone missing in the house break-in, because he'd put it back before she'd noticed it missing.

Pleased with himself, he left and headed home to wait for her call.

#

Tayla called the detective and ran her theory by him. She couldn't decide if he believed her or not, but she didn't care. In her heart, she knew. The detective said he would be meeting with them all at the museum. Things needed to be cleared up. Questions needed to be answered. There was still the matter of Stan's murder. He believed the break-in at her house to be connected to it, but he hadn't figured out how.

"What did the detective say?" Meredith asked.

"Nothing much. He will be meeting with us later this week," Tayla replied.

"I thought he was coming in tomorrow."

"Because of the break-in, he changed his plans."

"Did you just pout?"

"What? Me? No. Why do you ask?" Meredith twirled her hair.

"You are pouting. Oh. My. God. You like him."

"Don't be ridiculous. I just want him to catch Stan's murderer and figure out who broke into your house."

Tayla laughed. She knew when Meredith lied to her. Her voice got higher, she played with her hair, and she rocked as she spoke. She couldn't believe she didn't notice her attraction to him before. "Okay, you keep telling yourself that."

Meredith waved her hand to dismiss her and giggled.

"If it isn't the detective, then it's Zet. I saw you grinding with him on the dance floor. And he seems to be interested in you too. Looks like your dance card is full. No pun intended."

"Seriously, Tay. We were just having some fun. And he's into my ink. He noticed right away that it was the stela of the goddess Neith. He even commented that the queen married to Djzet had that same tattoo and her name was MerNeith."

"That's impressive. I didn't think that he was interested in anything, except getting out of work. He barely does anything. Well, except flirt with you."

Meredith blushed. "Well, he did ask me out a couple of times, but we never managed to connect, except for on the dance floor. Something always came up. My brother's accident, and then your break in. Stan's murder. The list just goes on."

"And there is Detective Flanagan. You're into him."

"Don't be ridiculous. Let's talk about you and Dene."

"We talked about that the other night."

"You briefly touched on the subject. Then everything went to hell."

"There's nothing more to say."

"There's plenty more to say. You told me you have a connection to him. Why? What makes him so special?"

Tayla started pacing. How could she answer that? She barely knew Dene. Yet the attraction was powerful. Every time he was near, she had an intense desire to be with him. It bordered on being obsessive. Even thinking about him got her aroused. She didn't understand the connection herself.

"You're going to wear a hole in the rug if you don't stop. What's going through your head?"

"I'm confused. I just ended things with Bennett. I don't know if I should jump into another relationship so soon. And I have no idea how long Dene will be here."

"Tay. Does he make you happy?"

"Well—"

"You're blushing. Talking about him makes you smile. Your relationship with Bennett ended long before you ended it. This is your subconscious telling you to move on. Go for it."

"Maybe. I'm going to wait and see if he acts on it. I don't want to be that girl."

"What girl?"

"You know, the one who has to be in a relationship."

"You aren't that girl. Besides, you wouldn't sleep with just anyone. There must be something there."

#

Dene could not believe what he had seen. He had only met him once, but if his memory served him correctly, the man in Tayla's house tonight was Bennett. Could he be the one who ransacked her home? Why would he do that? Dene rubbed the coin in his pocket. He could not say anything or Tayla and the police would know he was there. But what if he came back again? Would Tayla be in danger?

Maybe he had it incorrect. Maybe Bennett went to her house for the same reason he had—to try and find out who had done this to her. That explanation fit much better. He loved her and needed to help. Dene reacted the same way.

He had to protect her. The protective feelings grew stronger every moment. How could he protect her from whomever was after her? It would not be long before the weighing ceremony. Zet would not pass and they would once again be in limbo. He would not be here for her, but Bennett would. Dene slumped onto the couch.

He saw her face. Her smile. She conducted herself as his queen had. A kind word for everyone. Always willing to help. The gods must truly hate him. Putting such a fine woman here for him, knowing that he could never have her. If only Zet could pass their final test.

How could he help Zet pass it?

He stood and paced the room. Hopeless. Utterly hopeless.

Dene would need to distance himself from her. Only interact at the museum. Keep her from falling deeper in love with him. She should not be with someone that would not be on this plane of existence. His breathing increased, and his hands started shaking. It was not fair.

At least he would see her at the museum. He could take solace in that.

He was not in the mood to see anyone, especially Zet. Dene went to his room and lay down. Sleep eluded him. His bed felt empty without Tayla. He wanted her. He remembered how she led him into her bed, how she made love to him. It reminded him of MerNeith.

Dene tossed and turned. He looked up several times, 12:32, 2:39, 4:21. Tired of looking at the clock, he threw off the covers and shuffled to the shower. He turned the water on as hot as he could stand it. His skin turned a bright red. Dene stood under the hard pulsing water, but it did nothing for him. His muscles still ached. A dull throb echoed in his head. Every thought, every breath, he thought about Tayla. He had stood in the shower so long, the water had turned lukewarm. He reached up and turned it off. Several things in this century amazed him. This was one of them.

The food on his plate sat there, untouched. He had no appetite. Even living with Zet and Siamun, he had no company. Perhaps it was for the better.

Osiris, Isis, and Anubis, I pray for you to hear me. I have not found my queen, but I have found someone whose company I enjoy. If it would be possible, I wish to spend my life with her.

Although he expected no reply, he had hoped they considered his prayer. It would not be wise to think so, but he had nothing more to lose. For the first time in more than four-thousand years, his heart beat for another. She made him feel alive. To have that taken away in a short time seemed cruel. Nothing could make-up for losing Tayla. If only she could be the one to break the curse. But it had to be Meredith. She looked like his queen. She bore her mark. Her name even resembled MerNeith's.

Dene dumped the food into the garbage disposal. Mechanical teeth took care of it. Another great invention. The world today had so many advantages that his time never had. What would it be like in the next century? That thought nagged at him. Zet's refusing to reform, to learn what would free them, would keep him from being with Tayla or reaching the afterlife.

Since he awoke early, he had time to walk to work. It would give him time to think, to plan his day. Before he left, he turned on the television. He enjoyed watching it. It provided vital daily information that he needed to get through the day. It amazed him that the picture box could get information to so many people at one time. Everyone talked about watching it.

#

Dene loved the crisp cool air of the city. They didn't have weather like this in Egypt. He walked down the streets, pausing to take everything in. He missed his home. Life had been much simpler back then. He took his role as King Djzet's adviser seriously. One mistake. One error, and it cursed him. Four-thousand years, and he was still atoning. And he saw no end to his half-existence in the near future. He could feel his strength waning. He was running out of time.

The walk to work took forty-five minutes. The sun came out and brightened his path, but did nothing for his mood. How would he be able to avoid close contact with Tayla? Especially when he wanted nothing more than to be near her. He used his security card to enter and made his way to the exhibit room.

Dene looked at his wrist clock, 7:47. Soon everyone would be there. He set up an easel in the corner with a sketch pad and pencils. That would keep him away from everyone, especially Tayla. The exhibit staff started coming in, one by one. Shalhoub, a few college students — he could not remember their names — the museum curator, even Zet. Maybe he finally got to him. Perhaps Zet could be taught.

"Where are Meredith and Tayla?" Zet asked. "They are always here when I get here."

"Well, when you get here at noon, everyone's here before you," Shalhoub replied.

"We have much to do today. Shall we get started?" Dene asked as he worked on a sketch in the corner.

How unlike Tayla to not be here. It is Monday. Everyone had the weekend off. This is the day she usually arrived around 4:30

a.m. He had met her here several times to work. Where was she? Neither she nor Meredith had entered. Was she okay? Did her intruder hurt her? Dene shoved his hand in his pocket and rubbed his coin, then paced around the room. A few minutes passed and the door opened. Meredith walked in first, followed by Tayla.

Dene breathed in deeply. He loved the smell of her perfume. It reminded him of his queen. So many things about her reminded him of MerNeith. The way she carried herself, her positive attitude, the way she cared about everyone, no matter their station. She had a pure heart.

Tayla looked pale. Her hands shook. Her voice wavered when she spoke.

"Tayla, are you all right?" Dene asked. She had only been in the room for a minute, and he could not keep from engaging her.

"Rough night. Don't worry about me. But I could use some help. I have some things in my office that I need help with. Mer? Dene? Siamun? Zet? Would you mind?"

Dene stood and walked to the door, holding it open for everyone. "I shall assist you."

Everyone agreed and they all made their way to Tayla's office. Tayla pulled out her key to open the door but froze in the doorway.

"What's wrong?" Meredith asked.

Tayla grabbed the door frame and started breathing rapidly. "My office." She barely got the words out.

"What about your office?" Siamun asked.

Dene pushed past Meredith, Siamun, and Tayla, halting at the door. "The door to her office has been pried open."

Tayla pushed the door open and looked inside, and then turned away. Dene looked inside as well. What he saw made him angry.

Meredith pulled out her cell. "I've called Detective Flanagan. He gave specific instructions that we are not to enter the room."

Michele Jones

CHAPTER EIGHTEEN

Tayla sucked in a deep breath and held it. Not again. The office had been ransacked. A quick survey of the room reveled more of the same. Rose petals and stems on the floor. Just like she found them at the house. Furniture damaged. Drawers pulled out. Papers everywhere. The only thing different — a vase of roses in the center of her desk with a blood red envelop in front of it. She let out her breath, then started breathing rapidly. Her hands shook. Bile formed at the back of her throat. Who could have done this? Why her? Did someone hate her this much? Someone wanted her scared. But why?

Tayla turned away from her office. "Meredith said the detective told us not to touch anything. We shouldn't stay here. Let's go to the cafeteria and wait for the detective. Besides, I need to hit the vending machines. And get a large coffee."

Everyone agreed.

Dene offered her his arm, and she took it. They followed Zet and Meredith down the hall. Something about him made her feel calm, relaxed. And she needed that. Thoughts swirled thought her mind. If she had come in earlier as she had planned — would she be here now? Would she have startled her intruder? She shuddered at that thought.

The halls were quiet. The museum day hadn't started yet. The aroma of coffee pierced the hall as they got closer to the cafeteria. Inside, the room was empty. Too early for even the morning coffee crowd. Tayla headed straight for the vending machine. She fed it a few dollars, got two bags of M&Ms, and dropped them inside her purse. Then she went to the counter and got a large coffee.

She mindlessly wandered to one of the large tables in the back, threw down her candy, and slumped into the chair.

Tayla sipped her coffee, meanwhile she opened the M&Ms and sorted them.

The rest of the exhibit crew sat one by one, with coffee and snacks, as they waited for the detective. No one spoke. Each of them looked around the table, waiting for someone to say something.

The silence was disrupted by the echoes of clanging pots and pans. Not able to take it any longer, Tayla slid back from the table. "I need another coffee. Anyone else want one?"

Murmurs of no went around the table.

#

Dene had decided earlier that he would not engage with Tayla. Not even five minutes after she came in, he had broken his own rule. He could not stop himself. If she needed something, he ached to get if for her. When she suffered distress he needed to provide aid. Being around her made him feel alive. Something he had not felt in thousands of years. He shook his head. Time to make a break. He need to concentrate on anything other than Tayla. When she returned, he rose from his seat to examine the food offerings. After selecting a cinnamon pastry, he went to the coffee station and poured himself a bold, strong, coffee. The aroma scintillated his senses.

The coffee and pastry were the distraction that he needed. Dene enjoyed the dark beverage they called coffee. Something else he would miss when his time expired in this century. Beer and wine had been served at most meals in Egypt, and when someone fell ill, an herbal tea. Strange how things had changed in many ways since his birth, and even during the many centuries of trials to get to the afterlife.

He tore off a piece of the cinnamon pastry he had chosen and dipped it into his coffee. Something he watched Siamun do many mornings. He had dipped fruit into honey, but never a food into a beverage. He could not understand what made this so appealing. Dunking only made the pastry soggy. Something he would not do again.

Tayla slid her chair closer to Dene. Sweat beaded on his upper lip. He rubbed the sweat from his palms onto the khaki pants Meredith helped him select. His head pounded to the beat of his heart. How could he possible stay clear of her when she sat so close to him? He tore off another piece of the pastry and shoved it into his mouth. He needed time to calm down, to think of a way to distance himself from her without hurting her. Nothing came to mind.

Dene watched Zet flirt with Meredith—an arm subtly wrapped around her shoulders. The other hand lay on top of hers. He smiled at her and spoke softly to her, assuring her that everything would be fine. He flashed that dazzling smile of his and gently rubbed her palm. If he were correct, she was the reincarnated queen and could break the curse. Always thinking of himself. Dene hated that he didn't love her but rather wanted her to break the curse. To Zet, she was the means to an end. To break the curse. Could he really be so cold and uncaring? How could he put on such a convincing act?

The people sitting around the table finally started making small talk. Their nerves seemed to be on edge.

Tayla's head snapped up. "I never thought to check any of the other offices. Maybe others were broken into as well."

"She's right," Meredith said. "Her office may not be the only one broken into."

#

Dene stood. "We must check to see if anyone else had their office broken into."

"I believe we should wait for the detective," Zet said.

Selfish. Of course Zet would want to wait for the detective. He had what he wanted. Sitting next to Meredith, he had her attention. Dene could just imagine what he was thinking. It would be how he could win her hand. Break the curse. There were others involved in this. Tayla was in danger. The others could be in danger as well. How many lives would he ruin just for his own selfish needs?

Before they had the chance to go anywhere, Meredith asked, "Do any of you think this could be related to the ancient curse?"

Dene could see Shalhoub's face turning red, and could hear his breathing increase.

Shalhoub pushed back from the table and stood. "There is no such thing as a curse. We are not grave robbers." He began pacing. "Why would you think such a thing?"

Meredith replied. "Think about it. Stan, the security guard."

Dene noticed Shalhoub flinch. He had hoped no one else noticed that.

"Then Tayla's house was broken into. Now her office."

"Don't forget the exhibit room. How it was broken into. Things were moved. And Meredith's brother's accident." Tayla added.

"You are impossible," Shalhoub said. "There. Is. No. Such. Thing. As. A. Curse."

Zet stood. "Shalhoub, grave robbing was punishable in many ways in Egypt. Death is only one possible outcome. Bad luck or illness is also something that can happen."

Of course Zet liked the idea of the curse. It took the focus away from him. He killed the security guard. Stan. His name was Stan. And Zet had made Dene rearrange the exhibit room. They moved things to Zet's liking.

"Anyone associated with disturbing a tomb is a target. The curse is not specific to the robbers. Archaeologists, museum curators, collection managers. All have a part in disturbing the tomb," Tayla said.

Dene had listened to the banter going on long enough. He slammed his hands down on the table and stood. "I do not believe in the curse. We should focus on something else."

Michele Jones

CHAPTER NINETEEN

Tayla hated how this was dividing them. Dene and Shalhoub didn't believe in the curse. She didn't, but she thought someone was using it to scare her—them. Meredith was on the fence, she wanted to believe, but Tayla knew deep down she didn't. And Zet. Well, he knew about the curse and the outcomes of it. But did he believe the curse was possible? She couldn't tell.

It occurred to her that Zet used the curse to get closer to Meredith. She couldn't put her finger on it, but she didn't trust Zet. She knew that he and Dene were friends, but… something was off. The friendship was not like the one she shared with Meredith. And she didn't think that Shalhoub trusted him, either. He acted like he was stuck with him. That he was doing a favor for someone. Not like Zet was a colleague. So many things simply didn't add up.

Why was Zet always around when something bad happened. Coincidence? She didn't believe in them.

The detective entered the cafeteria and cleared his throat. "Did I interrupt?"

Meredith was quick to answer. "No. We were discussing ancient Egyptian curses, and how what is happening could be related."

Shalhoub huffed. "Not everyone thinks we are cursed."

Tayla saw Meredith's cheeks turn red. Meredith lowered her head and looked away from Flanagan. Tayla swore she saw a slight smile cross her lips. Her mind drifted to the conversation they had the other night. She knew it. Meredith liked the detective. She let her think that she was interested in Zet. That explained why she called the detective directly and not the police department.

Note to self, discuss this with her later.

"I need you to come with me, Ms. Amari. I would like you to tell me if anything is missing from your office."

Tayla stalled. She wanted answers. "Did you open the letter? I need to know what's in it. Was it a threat?"

The detective turned to Meredith. "Perhaps you should come with her. She may need your help."

"Anything to help with the investigation, Detective."

Tayla noticed that Meredith jumped at the chance to go with them. Even though she hated what was happening, she hoped her friend would finally find someone. She thought she had found her true love, but that hadn't worked out. Her mind drifted to her night with Dene. She sucked in a deep breath and her palms tingled. She felt a connection to him. Everything about him intrigued her, and he made her feel something that she never felt with Bennett.

Oh my God. Bennett. Could he be in danger from her intruder? Their relationship was strained, but she had to warn him. She didn't want anything bad to happen to him. Another thing to add to her to do list.

The detective walked over to Meredith and extended his hand toward the door. "Ms. Nazari, would you and your friend please follow me? This shouldn't take too long."

Tayla saw the detective reach to put his arm on Meredith's back. She sensed his attraction to her. She turned toward Dene. "Are you coming with us? The office you share with Shalhoub and Zet may have been broken into, as well."

"Of course I shall accompany you. My hope is that this will all be over soon."

Meredith turned back and asked Dene and Shalhoub, "Are you coming?"

"We're right behind you."

#

Zet grabbed Dene. "A word."

Dene jerked his arm from Zet's grasp. He leaned in and said something to Tayla and then turned and whispered so only Zet could hear. "Do not grab me again. I do not belong to you. I am simply along to guide you, to teach you, so that you may pass the next test, and the weighing of the heart."

Tayla stepped away, but did not leave. Zet scowled. He continued the conversation in hushed tones. "Listen to me. You must keep Meredith away from that detective. She is our chance at lifting this curse. I almost have her. But he keeps showing up."

"She is not our only chance. You could have ended this curse by changing your ways. You have not learned anything in four thousand years. Now our time fades in this century, and you see Meredith as the answer."

Zet could feel his face heat up. He clenched his fists and breathed harder. "I am your king. You serve me. I will not put up with your insolence."

"And I have done everything in my power to assist you. I have worked with you. Showed you the way. You do not listen, and you have not learned. We will suffer this curse for eternity. Do not make it about Meredith. Just because you believe Meredith is a way out for us does not mean that she is or that she will fall in love with one of us. "Dene turned away and started stalking to the door.

Two large steps and Zet caught him. "I did not excuse you."

"We are done here. Follow us or stay. The choice is yours. But know this. Meredith left with the detective and has been alone with him while you keep us here. If she is truly the queen, you should hurry to her."

Zet stood motionless as Dene escorted Tayla out of the cafeteria. He hated this. He had tried the gods' way. He had not been successful. Forty-two heart weighing ceremonies. Forty-two failures. There were only forty-three tests. If he failed this time, he would be forced to start over. More tests. More lessons. More trying to appease the gods. He managed to learn several of the gods' secret names, but not all. Starting the process all over again would be devastating. No, he would not let his chance of freedom slip by. He would win her favor. She would free him from this insufferable curse.

He needed to come up with a plan. But he also needed to get to her now. She left with the detective. They were alone. He needed to do something about that detective. What? Kill him? No. That would not work. He needed to keep him away from Meredith. That was the key. If he kept him away, she would think he did not like her and come back to him. Plan formed, now to execute.

#

Tayla walked beside Dene. But he wasn't the same Dene from the other night. He seemed distant. Was it something she did? Maybe something Zet said. They did just have words.

"Are you okay?" she asked.

"I am fine. Just thinking."

"About?"

"Nothing. Everything. Zet."

"I'll help if you let me."

"Do not worry about me. We must find out who is trying to hurt you."

"We don't know that someone is trying to hurt me. All we know is that someone broke into my house and my office."

"Are you not afraid?"

"At first, yes. I was. But the more I think about it, I'm pissed off."

"I do not understand. Pissed off?"

"Sorry, I'm angry."

"You need to be careful. At the very least, someone is trying to frighten you."

They discussed the break-in at her home and office. She had a feeling the break-ins were only a start. Was someone after something at the museum? But why her home? What did they expect to find? She had no enemies that she could think of. Did Stan try to keep them from stealing? Is that why he was killed? So many questions. No answers. It had only been a couple days, but she had hoped the police would know something.

They had reached her office. Looking around, she saw several officers. More than she thought necessary for a simple break-in. The detective knew something, and he wasn't sharing.

"Detective—"

Meredith pulled her aside. "Your office wasn't the only one broken into. My office, the curator's, the office that Shalhoub, Dene, and Zet use. All have broken into. Even the security office."

Tayla sucked in a deep breath. "Any other offices?"

"No. Only the offices of people tied to the Egyptian exhibit," Meredith replied.

"Any clues? How did they get in? This is a secure building."

"The building is secure, but there are no security cameras in the office area."

Tayla wanted to find anything, any clue as to who did this. The hall looked like it always did. There were no windows, no obvious footprints. Of course she was no detective, but surely there must be some clue.

The detective came over to her. "My men will not be finished processing the scene for some time. I'm going to need you to check things out when we finish. Let me know if anything is missing."

"Of course. Would it be possible for us to continue working? We have a lot to do to get the exhibit open."

"You can. For now." He addressed all of them. "I'm going to need statements from all of you. Don't leave until you've talked to me."

Meredith sauntered over to him. "Now do you believe us? This could be related to the curse of the mummy's tomb."

Shalhoub huffed. "There is no curse. This is a coincidence."

"I don't believe in coincidences." Tayla said. "Everything happens for a reason."

"I do not believe this is because of a curse," Dene said. "I think this could be someone putting us on. A joker, yes?"

The detective cracked his knuckles. "That's one heck of a theory. Murder is not a joke. And neither is breaking and entering. And Ms. Nazari's brother's accident. I didn't find any of those things funny."

"I did not mean to make light of the situation," Dene said. "I merely wanted to suggest an alternative to the curse. Please forgive me."

Tayla paced and threw her hands in the air. This—this person is disrupting all our lives. We need to find him. Get him off the streets. No more people getting hurt. No more break-ins. What do you need from us, Detective?"

Meredith came over to Tayla, and pulled her aside. "We need to talk."

Michele Jones

CHAPTER TWENTY

Tayla told Dene that she needed to talk with Meredith and would meet him back at the exhibit hall in five minutes. He nodded and walked off with Shalhoub and Zet. Tayla noticed that there was still some friction between Dene and Zet. Whatever they whispered about, it must have rubbed Dene the wrong way.

Meredith played with her hair. She twirled it around her finger, then pulled it back. Repeatedly. "Tay." Her voice cracked when she spoke. She paced up and down the hall, stopping in front of her office, and rocked back and forth.

Tayla came over to her and put her arm around her shoulder, spinning her so they faced each other. "What's wrong?"

"Nothing's wrong. I'm so confused. Remember the other night when we were talking?"

"We talked about a lot of things. Refresh my memory."

She threw her hands in the air. "The night we spoke about the curse."

"What about it?"

"I've been thinking about what you said. About the curse. So I called my brother to ask him about his accident. He didn't remember much, just that someone cut him off, forcing him off the road. I think you may be right. Someone is using that curse to scare us. But for the life of me, I don't know why."

Tayla hugged her. Then she placed her hands firmly on Meredith's shoulders and looked her square in the eyes. "Nothing is going to happen. Not to you, not to me. Not to anyone. Especially not with Detective Flanagan involved. I've seen the way he looks at you. He's not going to let anything happen to you."

Meredith blushed. "Do you truly believe he likes me?"

"Of course I do. I wouldn't say it if I didn't believe it."

"I feel different when he's around. I get this… feeling. My hands tingle, my heart beats faster. I can barely catch my breath. And I honestly can't think of anything else when he's around." She slumped against the wall. "You were right. I do like him."

"Did you tell him?"

"Did you tell Dene?"

Tayla rolled her eyes. Meredith was right. She liked Dene. They shared something. Some connection. But when they finished the exhibit? He would probably be gone.

"It's different with Dene. When the exhibit is up and running, he'll be gone."

"Give me a break. You slept with him. Besides, I barely know Shane, er, Detective Flanagan."

Tayla winced at the mention of sleeping with Dene. It was so much more than that. It was sensual. He made her feel—wanted.

Like she was the only person for him. But they hadn't connected since. She wanted him more than before. Touching her, loving her. She closed her eyes and could feel his body heat next to her. Saw those turquoise eyes looking at her. Taking her in. Exploring every inch of her. She shuddered. Her body jerked. "Dene's different than Detective Flanagan. Like I said, once the exhibit is done, he'll be gone."

A sadness washed over her. She didn't want him to leave. Bennett never made her feel this way. They connected in a way that was different than she had connected with anyone else. She felt whole when she was with him. Complete. Why did he have this effect on her? Maybe he would stay. With her. A smile crossed her lips.

#

Dene unlocked the exhibit room and sulked over to the easel he set up in the corner. He had to distance himself from Tayla. It had become more apparent than ever. Zet barely got by the last test the gods posed to him. But the gods knew he would not pass the weighing of the heart. Zet had not fooled them, not at all.

Even Zet did not have much better luck. He thought he had won Meredith. But that could not be further from the truth. It appeared Meredith was smitten with the detective. She deserved better than Zet. He used people. He was using her. If he had won her, he would have tossed her aside after the curse was lifted. The only person Zet cared about was Zet.

Shalhoub crossed the room to get away from Zet. "What do you think the detective will find? Do either of you know who's doing this? Tell me it wasn't either of you. I don't want to be involved in this."

"Silence. We are not involved in any of this petty foolishness." Shalhoub flinched.

Dene listened as Zet and Shalhoub argued back and forth. If Zet did not get his way, he could ruin Shalhoub's life. He forced him to help cover up the murder of that innocent security guard. His time was running short. He would fail the weighing ceremony, the gods would not be fooled by his insincerity. But he was relying on Meredith — his reincarnated queen. He believed he had won her heart. But he had not. She was interested in the detective.

Dene had no better luck. Meredith, who looked so much like his queen, did not capture his heart. Tayla did. In four thousand years, he had not felt this way. He hated this insufferable curse.

"You must lower your voices. The girls should be here at any time." Dene turned back to his easel.

Zet crossed the room and faced Dene. "Why do you not go after the girl. You want her."

"Because I do not want to hurt her. Our time is running out."

"Pfft. That does not matter. If you want her, take her. As I will do with Meredith."

"She does not want you. She wants the detective. You have doomed us to an eternity of hell on earth. A few months every century. That is not enough. I wish to be free of this curse. When will you learn?"

"Hey, guys. Don't let us interrupt," Tayla said.

"You are not interrupting. We are discussing the exhibit. The children's section. The hieroglyphs that Shalhoub wanted me to paint."

"That's not what it sounded like to us," Meredith replied.

Tayla walked over and looked on Dene's easel. "Your canvas is blank."

Dene rubbed the coin in his pocket. Close. She was too close. He had to get away from her.

#

Bennett paced his office. Tayla still hadn't called him. He trashed her house — no call. So he decided to trash the offices at the museum. Still nothing. He even left her and the others notes. He ran his hands through his hair. Why hadn't she called?

He needed to escalate his plans. Go to her parents. After that, Meredith's. That would definitely get her attention. She belonged to him.

The phone in his pocket vibrated. He hurriedly pulled it out. The voice on the other end wasn't her. "Doctor Coldwell."

They talked for a while, and he planned to meet her later that evening. Just because Tayla didn't want him today didn't mean he would spend the evening alone. He had needs.

Before he met the good doctor, he called from the burn phone that he bought and arranged for another rental car. He needed to get everything in place for the next round. He logged into the hospital computer and checked. Tayla's parents had a doctor appointment on Thursday. That worked out for him perfectly, he worked second shift at the hospital.

Two hours before he would meet Doctor Coldwell. Plenty of time to do a little shopping. He needed a few things for his visit to the Amari's. Dressing down was important. He couldn't risk anyone noticing him. Thirty-five minutes later he crossed the town line into Jeanette. He passed several small shops, but he wanted a large department store. Somewhere he would blend in and not be noticed.

After getting what he needed, he got back in the car and returned home. He had a date to get ready for.

Michele Jones

CHAPTER TWENTY-ONE

Zet stood by the door. He wanted to leave, but he knew he could not or things would go badly for him with the detective. How much longer would he have to wait for him? Would he ever come to the room to speak with them? To ask his questions? This century differed so much from the others. So much had changed.

Footsteps. Finally. The detective would come in and ask his questions. Most likely the same ones he had asked before. And his answers would be the same as they had been before. He did not do it. He did not know who could have done it.

A knock at the door. Zet never moved. Someone else would get the door. It was not his place. He was a king. A god. All pharaohs had servants. He directed Dene to answer the door.

#

Tayla looked at Meredith when the detective entered the room. A glow radiated from her, and a smile played on her lips. She didn't move, but she rocked back and forth, playing with her hair. Oh, yeah, she liked him.

"Is there somewhere we can talk in private?" the detective asked.

"We can set something up at the back of the exhibit. Will that work for you?" Tayla replied.

"Yes, that'll do."

"Dene. Would you mind? I could use your help. Detective, Zet, Siamun. I could use you as well. We'll move that table over there to the back of the hall. Meredith and I will grab the chairs."

Zet never moved. He watched the others do the work. Tayla shook her head. He was useless. Only worked limited hours. Never on time. How could he possibly know anything? She would suggest he go first so that he could leave.

#

Zet approached the detective. "May I make a suggestion?"

"Go on," the detective replied.

"Where I come from, men let women go first. I propose that you interview the Ms. Amari and Ms. Nazari first. I wish to show them the respect that we show the women where I come from."

"Ladies first. I like it."

Before either woman could protest the detective said, "Ms. Amari, come with me."

Dene walked over to Zet and whispered, "What was that all about? You never in your life put a woman first or anyone for that matter."

Zet felt his face grow hot. It took all his self-control not to strike Dene. "I always put my queen first. That was proper."

"You never did. That is why she turned to me. And I to her. Your actions caused this entire debacle. And I suspect an ulterior motive behind your noble intentions."

"No motive. I am trying to put my lessons to use. To show that I have learned." How could Dene be so suspicious? He could not have been that transparent. He wanted Meredith away from the detective. Once the girls were finished, he planned to volunteer to go next. Then he could meet them and discuss the exhibit. Get closer to Meredith.

The exhibit. Tayla and Meredith put together a nice exhibit showcasing him. He appreciated that. But he needed to keep Meredith away from the detective. He could not risk losing her. In four thousand years, he had not passed the weighing of the heart ceremony. Neither he nor Dene had been able to win the queen's heart. This was the closest they had been. He would not risk that. If the detective continued to pursue Meredith, he would have to take matters into his own hands.

The detective chose Tayla first. That left Meredith for him. Zet went and sat beside her. "I am sorry this is happening to you, to all of us."

"It's not your fault. Someone is trying to scare us. But for the life of me, I don't know why."

He reached and took her hand. "Are you frightened?" Meredith squeezed his hand. "No. No, I'm not. I'm angry. This — this asshole needs to be caught before he actually hurts someone."

"I will stay close to you. Protect you."

She squeezed his hand. "That's sweet of you, but you don't have to worry about me. I'll be fine."

Zet wanted to continue the conversation, but the detective came over. "Ms. Nazari, you are next. Ms. Amari asked that when each of you finish, you meet her in the cafeteria."

After the detective and Meredith left, Dene came over and sat by Zet. "You are truly something."

"Thank you. I am glad you realize that."

"That was not meant as a compliment. You—"

"Look at him. He is trying to win her favor. She belongs to me. She is my queen. I need her to break this curse. Something needs to be done about him."

"I knew you had other motives. She does not belong to you. Instead of trying to scheme your way into the afterlife, try being honest, noble, fair, kind. Your lack of compassion for anyone but yourself is the reason we have been cursed."

"You are hardly innocent, Dene."

"One indiscretion. And believe me I have paid for it. For over four thousand years, I have paid for it."

#

Tayla sorted her M&Ms—brown, red, yellow, orange, blue, green—and sipped her coffee. Could the detective be right? Would this person go after her family? Her friends? Even her coworkers? What did he want?

Even though Meredith had her own office, she was always in Tayla's. They did most of their work together. It never occurred to her that Meredith could be next. But she was targeted, too. Rose petals and stems all over her office. And she had the flower arrangement and note just like hers. Did the notes say the same thing? She wondered.

Tayla had already eaten the brown and red M&Ms and had started eating the yellow when Meredith walked in.

"It's a wonder you're as thin as you are the way you've been eating M&Ms lately. You've got to relax."

"I'm relaxed."

"Really? If you were, you wouldn't be on the yellow M&Ms. This is getting to you."

"What if the detective's right and he goes after our families? Could I have avoided all of this? Did I do something to cause this?"

"Tay, whoever's doing this is a sick, twisted maniac. You didn't do anything to cause this. None of us did."

Tayla's stomach lurched and her hands shook. "I've got to call Bennett. He needs to know he could be in danger."

"I'll call him. You don't need that kind of stress right now."

"No. I owe him that much."

"Fine. He probably won't answer anyway."

She made the call. "Bennett. Sorry to bother you but, when you get a chance, give me a call."

"Told you he wouldn't answer. He probably won't call back. Self-centered, asshole."

"Mer. That's not nice."

"Really? And the way he treated you these last few months was? He's not on my favorites list."

Tayla's phone rang Bennett's ring tone. She hesitated, then answered. He needed to know. She gave him a quick overview, then hung up.

"Well? What did he have to say?" Meredith asked.

"He thanked me for my concern. Said he's worried about me. Said he'd call later, he had to go. He was busy."

"Jerk."

"Mer, please. He doesn't owe me anything. We're not a couple. He's trying. At least he called back. I didn't know if he would after how things ended." She knew Meredith wanted her to have nothing to do with him. But she had to let him know. Even though they weren't a couple, she needed to warn him. She did what she needed to do.

Time went by slowly. Tayla looked at her watch. Thirty minutes passed, but it felt like hours. What could the detective possibly be asking them? They needed to get beyond this and back to work. Maybe she could get something done with Meredith while they waited. She reached for another M&M, but didn't have any left. Noise came from the hall, and Zet walked in. Behind him. Bennett.

Tayla didn't know what to do. Why did he come? Could he really be that concerned about me? Old feelings stirred. They had a history. She couldn't deny that. Five years they were together.

The two walked over to the table and sat down. If looks could kill. Meredith stared him down.

"What are you doing here?" Meredith asked Bennett.

Bennett ignored Meredith and turned to Tayla. "Can we talk?"

Tayla sighed. It took something like this to make him think about her. Come to her. At least he cared a little. She would give him that much. "I have a few minutes before I have to get back. She stood and walked to another table, leaving Meredith and Zet.

#

Dene walked in the cafeteria and saw Zet and Meredith sitting together. But Tayla was not with them. He looked for her. Sitting at a small table in the back of the cafeteria, he saw Tayla with Bennett. His face grew hot and his hands shook. But he had no right to be jealous. She did not belong to him. Soon he would not be around at all. She deserved a chance at happiness.

But he did not trust Bennett. He had no idea why. Perhaps because he reminded him of Zet, selfish and self-centered.

Looking over, he saw Tayla smiling. She even held his hand. More reason for him to distance himself from her. Truth be told, he hated seeing her with him. He had hurt her before, and there was no reason to believe that he would not hurt her again. But he respected her decisions, and if Bennett was what she wanted, he would not stand in her way, no matter how badly it hurt him.

Thoughts ran through his head at the speed of light. Would Zet be able to pull it off? Get Meredith to break the curse by being with him. He watched Zet interact with her. Touching her—tracing her tattoo. She did not brush him off, but she did not respond as a lover would. She did not care for him in that way.

Meredith and Zet were a mere distraction for him. His main concern was Tayla and Bennett. What were they talking about? Did he win her back? Dene could not help but stare over at the two of them. Tayla laughed and brushed a stray strand of hair out of her eyes.

The room got hotter by the second.

Dene selected a beverage and a snack. He stood in the middle of the cafeteria trying to decide where he should sit. His feet did not move. He wanted to go over and sit beside Tayla. She would be gracious and let him, but it would not be right. And if Zet was having any luck with Meredith, he did not want to intrude. He did have a third option, a table of his own. Meredith saw him before he sat at the closest table and waved him over. He knew then, Zet had no chance with her. Soon he would have only a memory from this time to console him.

And another unfulfilled love.

Michele Jones

CHAPTER TWENTY-TWO

Tayla had been given the okay to go back into her house a few days ago. In one way she couldn't wait—in another way, she was apprehensive. Her family had helped her clean up the mess, put everything back in order. What if the intruder came back? It took days to clean up the mess the intruder left. And the note that came with the flowers? The detective hadn't told her the contents of the note. Said that he would after the lab examined it. She feared he didn't want her to know what it said. How could someone be so filled with hate? Both she and Meredith had been threatened. The detective worried about their safety. He assigned a detail to ensure their security. But could he? Hopefully, she would not have to test that theory.

Tayla stared out the window. Three news vans parked out front. Two reporters getting set up, the third walking toward the building. This was bad. Not only for the museum, but for her. She could just hear the lecture from her parents now.

"It's not safe. You and Meredith shouldn't stay alone. You should stay with us." Even though she could take care of herself, she would never be able to convince them of that. To them, she would always be a little girl.

Things at the exhibit had stalled. They couldn't get anything done. Everyone was on edge. Looking over their shoulders. No one believed they were cursed. They all thought someone had something against the museum, or against her. But she honestly couldn't think of anyone who would want to hurt her.

Meredith refused to play the victim. Staying home was against her nature. She had wanted Tayla to go out with her, but she declined. After Meredith left, she called her parents. The silence on the other end of the phone spoke volumes. When her mother finally spoke, Tayla could hear the fear in her voice. When she closed her eyes, she could see her mother shaking. After an hour on the phone—more than half of it assuring them she would be fine—she hung up.

It was time to go back to her house. Everything had been restored to normal, before the break in. Time to resume her life. Meredith was right. No more being a victim.

Tayla paced around the living room, looking at her phone. No one called, no one texted. The evening dragged on. She turned on the television, but didn't really watch anything. She stood up, she sat down. She looked out the window, she looked at her phone. The detective had kept his word. Police cars drove around the neighborhood.

The phone call to her parents did nothing to alleviate her irritation about what had happened. She clicked through the food channels, the home and garden channels, the shopping channels.

Nothing held her interest. She needed to relax. She wanted to be at work early tomorrow. They had so much to do to get the exhibit open to the public. With things strained because of everything that happened, she would have to be the one to bring order to that chaos. She wasn't tired. Maybe a glass of wine. Something to take the edge off. Then she would be off to bed.

It was just what the doctor ordered. She felt relaxed, so she went to her room. After setting her alarm, she'd read a little bit, then go to sleep. Her eye lids grew heavy a few pages in. Tayla closed her book, reached up, and shut off the light.

Four in the morning, her alarm went off. Tayla got up and took a hot shower. She stood under the massaging shower head and let the water pulse on her achy muscles. The hot water and the pulsing shower head felt amazing. Fifteen minutes later she stepped out of the shower and dried off. She was ready to face the day.

As she got dressed, she made a list of what she wanted to get done. The children's part of the exhibit was her top priority. If the children got engaged, the exhibit would be successful. Something her mentor had taught her. And kids loved touching things. Her design would let them do that. And they would get the real Egyptian experience—sand, heat, and all. As an added bonus, they would enter the children's part of the exhibit through a sarcophagus. She had it planned down to the most minute point. An easy to find, but supposedly hidden release. Part of the exhibit even had the kids building a small pyramid. Who said learning couldn't be fun?

She shoved her notes in her back pack and grabbed her car keys. Before she went outside, she looked around. Tayla didn't think she would see anyone, but she promised her parents she would be extra careful. All clear. She made it to work in fifteen minutes. Going in early had its perks. Light traffic. And she got primo parking when she went in this early. She swiped her card key and entered the building.

Since the break-in, Tayla had a temporary office, and she shared it with Meredith. It worked, for now. But she couldn't wait to get back in her office where she had what she needed.

There was a knock at her door. "Security."

Tayla's heart pounded fast, and her breathing sped up. She looked around for anything she could use to protect herself. If she were in her office, she would have that baseball bat her dad gave her. The only thing she could find in here was a yard stick. She reached in her purse and took out her perfume. If nothing else, she could momentarily blind an attacker, long enough to get away — at least she hoped she could.

"Door's open. Let yourself in."

The knob turned slowly. Tayla held her breath, waiting for the guard to enter. The door opened slower than the knob turned. "Ms. Amari?"

Tayla let out her breath. "Yes, John."

"What are you doing here?" John asked.

"There's a lot to do to get the exhibit up and open to the public. And the break in put us behind. I'm just trying to get back on schedule."

"Sorry to bother you. But I saw the light and had to check. I'll let you get back to work."

"No bother, John. Better safe than sorry."

After loading her cart with supplies from the supply room, Tayla made her way to the exhibit room and got to work. She taped off where she wanted the sarcophagus secret passage for the entry. Then she set up a table and started laying out supplies for the kids.

#

Dene could not sleep. Shalhoub was up talking to his family, and he had no idea where Zet had gone. Usually the television relaxed him, but not tonight. The past two days were long and rough. He had to work closely with Tayla, but he managed to keep his distance. He only acted in a professional manner. He did not eat lunch with her, he took separate breaks. If everyone left the room, he did too. Being alone with her was not an option.

It was difficult. He longed to be near her. He was drawn to her. The room came alive when she entered. And she made a point to be near him. The closer she got, the more connected he felt. She was beautiful, inside and out. And the perfume she wore drew him closer.

Damn, why couldn't she be the one? Dene cursed the gods. And Zet.

He went to the kitchen, made himself a hot tea, and drank it quickly. Tayla filled his every thought. Dene shook his head to clear his mind. After putting his half-full cup into the sink, he went to his bedroom.

It was empty. Dene tugged his shirt and jeans off, and crawled into bed. It lacked the warmth he had when he shared Tayla's bed. He turned on the radio—a great invention—and listened to soft music. His muscles still tensed. He tossed and turned, reaching for someone that was not there. Time passed, slowly—1:24— 3:12—4:01. He rolled out of bed and opened his window, letting in the early morning air. It did nothing to relax him.

Going back to bed would be futile. He took a quick shower, dressed, and left for work. At least the walk would help clear his head. The brisk morning air was among the many things that he would miss. This century had come a long way from the previous, and Dene imagined that the next century would be even more amazing. The phone with no cord. Motorized cars. Buildings taller than the pyramids, built by machines.

If Zet would have learned anything from his lessons — humility, compassion, kindness — the gods may have removed the curse. But Zet did nothing to help either of them. Dene rubbed the coin in his pocket and picked up his pace. At least he would get something done on the exhibit before anyone — Tayla — got there. Those green eyes haunted him. And her perfume, he could still smell it, and it had been days.

A horn blared. He had not been paying attention and walked out into the path of a car. He put up his hands and mouthed the words "I am sorry" to the angry driver. Dene needed to be more careful. He was not immune to the human element. If he were to be injured, he would feel the pain. He could also be killed. That would only end his torture in this century. He would be back for the next one.

Anubis, Isis, Osiris, why? Had he not tried? Would they ever forgive him his indiscretion? He cursed Zet as he continued to the museum. Then he heard the gods speak to him.

Do not despair. Things are not as bad as you perceive. Believe that you are on the right path. Follow your heart.

He looked around, but saw nothing. The gods did not often speak to him. But when they did, why must it be so cryptic? He looked at his wrist clock — 5:13. He pulled out the security card and the key from his pocket. After swiping his way inside, he headed to the temporary office he shared with Zet and Shalhoub. Sketch pad and chalks in hand, he headed to the exhibit. He would have at least two hours before anyone else showed up. He would sketch the hieroglyphics on the wall and be ready to start painting later in the day.

Dene opened the door and halted. Tayla knelt on the floor near the entrance to the children's part of the exhibit. He started walking toward the easel he had set up in the corner. Why was she here this early? He had been coming in early all week, and no one had come before 8:30. He started breathing faster. He turned to leave, but Tayla stopped him.

"Dene, you're here early."

"As are you."

"I couldn't sleep, so I thought I could get some work done."

Dene turned and started toward the door.

"Where are you going?"

"I will leave you to your work. I do not want to be in your way."

"Don't be ridiculous. You won't be in my way."

Her scent filled the room. "If you are sure." He walked along the perimeter of the room. He could not risk getting too close to her, his self-control already waning. She got to him. His muscles hardened, his breathing already faster than normal. He could feel his face heating up.

Tayla rose and stomped over to his easel. "Why have you been avoiding me?"

"I am not avoiding you."

"Could have fooled me. You never talk to me anymore. You haven't eaten with us all week."

"I have just been busy working on my part of the exhibit." Her perfume tickled his nose. He backed away from her. She moved closer.

"I thought we had something. I—I—thought you and I…" Her voice trailed off.

His throat tightened. "What did you think?"

"The other night. We made love. I thought… Never mind." She turned and hurried back to the children's part of the exhibit.

How could he be so insensitive? She was in pain because of what he did. He dropped his things at the easel and went to her. "I saw you with your boyfriend the day our offices were broken into. I am glad you were able to reconcile."

Her cheeks got red. She threw her hands in the air. "I was warning him. I told him about the break-ins. That he could be a target, because of his connection to me. We aren't a couple. That's over."

"You were holding hands, laughing. You looked like you belong together."

She raised her voice and waved her hand in the air. "I don't love him. I love you." She raised her hand to cover her lips.

Dene stood there, looking away from her, at the wall he was to paint. He did not know what to say. He knew what he saw, and it looked like she and her ex-boyfriend were together again. Could she truly love him? Perhaps he should try. "Tayla, I—"

He did not have time to finish, when he looked up, he saw Tayla leaving the room.

Dene did not move. What should he do? Should he go after her? Would she even want him too? How could he let this happen?

Seconds passed, he made his decision. He would tell her everything. He ran out the door. The hall was empty. Which way? He hesitated, where would she go? He ran left, hoping to find her. The hall led to the cafeteria. He yanked the door open, and ran inside. Empty. He guessed wrong. He spun around, left, and headed to the temporary offices. He tugged on her door, but it was locked. He could see light coming from underneath. "Tayla, please. Let me in."

She did not open the door. He pounded on the door. "We need to talk. Please."

He could hear footsteps, and the deadbolt clicked, but she did not open the door.

Dene hesitated. How much should he tell her? The thought of hurting her more raged in his head. He inhaled deeply, pushed the door slowly, and walked in.

Michele Jones

CHAPTER TWENTY-THREE

Tayla sat behind her make-shift desk, her back to the door. For the life of her, she didn't know why she unlocked the door. His actions made it clear that he wasn't interested in her. She told him she loved him, and he just stood there. No response. Even Bennett would have said something.

She knew Dene came in, she could smell his cologne. Her body betrayed her. Goosebumps trickled up her arms, down her neck. Why did she respond to him like that? And what could he say that would change his earlier actions?

She could hear his footsteps. The closer he got, the stronger his cologne scent grew. She closed her eyes and inhaled deeply, trying to commit the smell to memory. He might never get that close again.

A light touch brushed her shoulder. It lit her skin on fire and her heart beat faster. God she wanted him. What was wrong with her? She pushed back from the desk, and rose, still not facing him. The hand once again touched her shoulder, and spun her gently around.

"You must listen to me, let me explain."

"There's nothing to explain. Your actions spoke volumes."

"I do not understand. I did not do anything."

"Exactly. You just stood there. I felt like such a fool." Her heart beat faster with each word she uttered.

"You are not a fool. You are everything I desire in a woman. Kind, compassionate, loving. But—"

"There it is. The but. But you don't love me. But I'm not good enough for you. But I can't be with you. But, but, but. Save it. I've heard it all before."

Dene grabbed her arm and pulled her to him. His touch sent chills up her spine.

"Don't. I can't take this. Not now."

"Be quiet and listen to me. There is something I must tell you. Something you need to understand about me."

Tayla threw his hand off of her and parked her hands on her hips. "Go on. Tell me."

Dene paced the room. She could see every breath he took, watched his jaw clench. She felt her cheeks grow hot. Not now. She didn't want him to see her blush. After a couple calming breaths to steady her voice, she said, "I'm waiting."

Dene stopped pacing and faced her. "I am not the person you think I am. I—" Dene jammed his hands in his pockets and started pacing again.

"You're what? Tell me."

Dene took both her hands in his. "I want you to promise me that you will listen to everything I have to say. Don't interrupt. Let me finish my story before you say anything. Do I have your word?"

Tayla fought to hold back a tear. Whatever he had to tell her couldn't be good.

"Your word."

"You have it."

"Do you remember the curse associated with king Djzet?"

She nodded.

"It is real. The pharaoh, his advisor, and the queen. They are reincarnated once a century, to atone for their sins."

"Come on. Are you—"

"You gave your word."

"Sorry. Please go on."

"Remember, you said you would hear my story to the end."

Tayla locked an invisible lock on her lips and tossed the invisible key over her shoulder. If he was going to tell a crazy story, then she could act like a child.

"Zet is the reincarnated pharaoh, and I am his advisor. We awakened the day the exhibit arrived. I have been guiding him since. When Zet passed, it was his desire that his queen and I be buried with him. And we were. As you know, upon death, the soul entered the underworld where it had to pass tests and then reach final judgment. Zet could not pass any of the tests. Anubis, Isis, and Osiris were angered. In all their years, Zet was the only pharaoh that could not pass their tests and enter the afterlife."

Tayla's eyes opened wide. Dene wanted her to believe that Zet was the reincarnated Djzet?

Dene paused and paced the room. Tayla saw a pained look on his face.

"Zet ruled unfairly and was cruel to everyone, including his sister, the queen. He used her, like he used so many. Once she bore him a child, he had nothing more to do with her. Often she was alone, and always she was sad. We became friends, as Zet left me to deal with her while he went off with one of his concubines. That friendship turned into love. We became lovers."

Tayla shook her head and crossed her arms across her stomach. She sucked in a breath and rocked back and forth.

"No one angers the gods and gets away with it. Zet had no redeemable qualities. When his deeds were weighed, the scales did not tip in favor of good. His bad deeds scale was so heavy, he should have been handed over to the Devourer of the Dead, or what you call hell. But Zet was given a second chance to atone and pass the tests. Because of my indiscretions with the queen, I had been tasked with teaching him how to pass all the trials. I have not succeeded.

His story was beyond belief, but she had to know. "Why you?"

"I had to atone for my indiscretions with the queen, and she had to atone as well. She was the lucky one. She has no recollection of what happens. She is reincarnated as we are, but she has no memory of the past."

"Is there no other way for the curse to be broken?"

"Yes, there is one other. If we should find the reincarnated queen and get her to fall in love with one of us, we shall spend the rest of our time on earth with her, and the other will live out his days to atone."

"Nice story. You don't actually expect me to believe it, do you?"

"It is the truth."

"Riiight. I can't believe you. If you aren't interested in me, you didn't have to make up a story. You could have just told me."

"You do not understand."

How could she have been so stupid? She couldn't believe she thought he was the one. Her hands shook. "You should leave."

"You said you would hear me out. Give me the chance to explain."

"I did. And you came up with this absurd tale. You must think I'm a real idiot."

"What can I do to convince you?"

Before he could say anything more, Meredith walked in.

"Hey. You're both here early. Getting an early start?" She winked at Tayla.

"Dene was just leaving. He has a lot to get done."

"Excuse me. I will see you at the exhibit." He turned and left.

Tayla slumped into her chair and put her head in her hands. First Bennett, now Dene. She had terrible taste in men.

"Something you want to tell me?"

"Headache, nothing to worry about." She would tell her everything, but not now. Besides, they had work to do.

#

Bennett parked down the street from Tayla's parents' house and got organized while he waited for them to leave. He knew it wouldn't be long, her dad arrived early everywhere they went.

He planned to use their key to get inside, and then he would break the door before he left. He wanted to be inside as quickly as possible, he didn't want to be seen. He would do what he needed to do and get out again.

Bennett knew Tayla had been worried about him. She called him to warn him about possibly being a target for a break in. She actually thought someone tried to make it look like she was being cursed. He smirked. He needed to keep up what he was doing, it worked. Soon, she would be coming back to him again. Once she learned that her parent's house had been targeted, she would call him. Then he would do Meredith's house. Hell, maybe he should fake a break-in at his own place. Then she'd really be worried for him. Come running back to his arms.

He rubbed his hands together, and cracked his knuckles. She belonged to him, and he would get her back.

The Amari's car drove right past him. Time to put his plan into action. He slung his backpack over his shoulder and walked up to the house. He rang the bell and waited a few seconds, just to be sure, then used the key he had made when he broke into Tayla's.

Once inside, he put his plan into action. He broke all the pictures, and threw torn apart flowers around the place, leaving stems on the floor, and petals scattered about. He needed to be consistent so that Tayla thought it was the same person. There would be no note here. He turned out several drawers, tore apart the furniture on the main floor, then went upstairs and did more of the same. Once he was satisfied with his handiwork, he left out the back door, making sure he broke the lock from the jamb.

He walked calmly to his car. Inside, he pumped his fist with satisfaction. "Oh, yeah. She'll be calling me."

He turned the car on and drove away. He had more work that needed to be done.

#

Dene did not know what to do. He heard her words echo in his head over and over. "I love you." Yet he did not respond. If he had, would things be different? Would he have had to tell her about his plight? Too late. He told her. And it ruined any chance he had with her. She did not believe what he said, she thought he played her for a fool. How could he convince her of the truth? Fate had once again dealt him a cruel hand.

He found it difficult to concentrate. He could not draw, and he did not dare try to paint. Neither Tayla nor Meredith had come in. That meant Tayla was telling Meredith everything. He knew that Meredith was her confidant. He paced around the room. Shalhoub was working on something in his corner, Zet decided not to show. His footsteps echoed as he paced. Would Tayla come in and work with him? Would she talk to him again? Did he have enough time left to have one last night with her?

The door opened, and Meredith walked in. She stomped over to him and faced him, staring at him. She raised her hand and slapped him across the face. "Tayla told me everything. How could you? She loved you. And you used her. Listen to me very carefully. Leave her alone. I won't have her hurt by you again."

Dene did not respond to her. Her words and her actions told him all he needed to know. Any chance he thought he had to be with Tayla was gone. Meredith made it clear, she wanted nothing to do with him.

Dene left the room and went to the cafeteria. He went through the line and grabbed whatever they served and placed it on his tray. It did not matter, he needed something in his stomach. He took his tray and sat facing the door. Perhaps Tayla would come in and he would have the chance to speak with her and explain. Several people came and left, but Tayla was not one of them.

He pushed his food around the plate. A bite or two was all he could force down. After disposing of his garbage and tray, he made his way back to the exhibit. After all, he had work to do.

Tayla, Meredith, and Shalhoub were all there, working together. He started over toward them, but the look he got from Meredith made him change his mind. He took the picture from his easel and the chalk, then started drawing on the wall. It was not his best drawing, but it would do.

Tayla's phone rang and all the color drained from her face. After she hung up, Dene overheard her telling Meredith that her parent's house was broken into.

Meredith spoke louder than Tayla. "You should leave, go see what you can do to help.

"I told them I would come right over, but they told me not to. The police are there, and they can't do anything."

Everyone got quiet.

About one-half hour later, Detective Flanagan walked through the door. "Ms. Amari, come with me please."

#

Tayla excused herself and went with the detective. Perhaps he had some answers. But if he did, why not share them with everyone. Things didn't make sense. She knew that anyone associated with the exhibit would be targeted, but she honestly didn't think whoever did this would go after her parents, or anyone's parents. She would have her answer soon enough.

"Ms. Amari, this could take a while. Let's sit in the cafeteria. We shouldn't be disturbed there."

"Of course. Anything to help with the investigation." They didn't speak again until they entered the cafeteria. Tayla headed for the vending machine for her usual bags of M&Ms and then went for a coffee. The detective poured himself a large black coffee and walked to a table in the back, away from everything. Tayla joined him and opened her M&Ms, sorting them as they spoke.

"Ms. Amari. We went over the security tapes from the break-in."

"Did you find something?"

"There are no cameras in the office area. There was no forced entry. However, we did check with security. Your card was swiped at 2:07 a.m. Is there something you wish to tell me?"

Tayla gasped. "I—That's impossible. John was here when I came in that morning. It wasn't me."

"Can you tell me where you were at 2:07 that morning?"

"I was asleep. At Meredith's. She can vouch for me." *Her stomach clenched. What in God's name was going on?*

"What about my parent's house? Any clues there?"

"We're still working the scene?"

"Do you have any leads?"

"I can't discuss that investigation with you, but I need to know if you can think of anyone who would want to do this? Is there anyone who had a grudge against your parents?"

"No. I can't think of anyone. My parents keep to themselves and are nice to everyone."

The detective asked a few more questions Tayla had no answer for, just like the break-in at her house. Then he changed the subject to the break-in at her house.

"The lab got the forensics back from the break-in at your house. We found sand in the bedroom and the living room."

"Oh, I can explain that. I had been working on the children's part of our exhibit—an interactive display. The pyramids of Ancient Egypt are surrounded by sand, so we set up our display with sand. I had been walking through it all day. I had it all though my clothes. I thought I got it all out, but I must have missed some."

"I see. Can you tell me where you got the sand?"

"We got it at Lowe's. Why?"

The detective simply nodded. "Did you get anything else for the exhibit from there?"

"Nothing out of the ordinary. Some lumber, a few large cinder blocks, some other building items. Tell me. Why are you asking these questions?"

"The sand that we found isn't regular play sand. Our lab tech said it is over four thousand years old. And it comes from ancient Egypt."

Tayla sucked in a deep breath. "How? What? That's not possible. Where did that come from? "

"I was hoping you could tell me."

"I have no idea."

"Is it possible for the items in the exhibit to have sand with them?"

Tayla was now eating the M&Ms at a much faster pace. She finished eating the yellow as he spoke and put all the orange into her mouth at once, leaving only the blue and green. "The exhibit items are all well cared for. They come in highly protected and would never have dirt of any kind on them. When they are displayed, they are kept behind protective glass, except the items that are not subject to the elements. There is no way for these items to have sand on them."

"I need you to be absolutely positive that isn't the case."

"I'm one hundred percent positive that isn't the case. We haven't even unpacked the majority of the items. We did an inventory the first couple days that items came in, and we did place a few of the smaller items, but the larger items are still in a climate-controlled storage area."

"I'd like to see the storage area."

"Follow me. We need to get Security, they have the key. There are protocols in place that must be followed. We also need to get Mr. Shalhoub, the collection's manager. He must be present if we are to search the exhibit items."

"Let's go."

Tayla and Detective Flanagan headed back to the exhibit hall at a brisk pace. Thoughts ran rampant in her head. Four thousand-year-old sand? Could it be? She shook her head. Maybe Dene told the truth. She couldn't wrap her head around that. She was letting her imagination get the better of her. She didn't believe in the curse of the pyramids, and she certainly didn't believe that Dene and Zet were the reincarnation of the Pharaoh Djzet and his advisor.

More things to think about. If Dene and Zet were the reincarnation of the pharaoh and his advisor, then the queen must be nearby. And if Dene was right, Zet believed Meredith to be the queen. The war in her head raged on full force. In her heart, she desperately wanted to believe Dene. But her head told her otherwise. Absurd. Absolutely, without a doubt, this couldn't be happening. Or could it? The answer she needed lay with Dene. She would have to talk to him. Possibly Zet. And she needed to protect Meredith from Zet, if the curse was indeed true.

They arrived at the exhibit and went inside. Dene had painted part of the wall with the curse, and Shalhoub stood beside him directing, guiding. But where had Zet gone? Once again, missing from the exhibit. Tayla questioned everything. If Dene was right, everything she knew, everything she believed, in would change. And she didn't think it would be for the better—especially for Meredith.

While they waited for Shalhoub to get his things, the detective's phone rang. He excused himself and stepped away, but still within earshot. His face grew red, and she could partially make out his conversation. What she couldn't hear, she could guess.

"What do you mean another break-in? Was anyone hurt?" The detective yelled into the phone and paced up and down the hall.

Tayla watched the detective's demeanor go from bad to worse. He didn't have an inside voice. He paced as he talked. She inched closer to hear more. The speaker on his phone must have been turned up the whole way. She could make out some of the conversation.

"No... Home... Townhouse alarm disabled... Front door busted open. He's cooperating fully," the female voice on the other end said.

"Give me an address, I'll check it out when I finish here."

Tayla heard the address on the other end, clear as a bell. The Village at Sweet Water. Bennett bought his townhouse there, last year. He loved it. New construction in the historic district and close to Downtown Pittsburgh and work. Was Bennett the latest victim? His only connection to the exhibit was Tayla. She could only imagine his anger at being a target. If they didn't catch the perpetrator soon, someone else would get hurt.

The detective ended his call and came back to Tayla just as Shalhoub walked out of the exhibit.

"I've gotta make this quick, I'm needed elsewhere."

CHAPTER TWENTY-FOUR

Zet knew his time was limited. His life force dwindled—and he was so close. How could he get Meredith to become his queen once again? Auburn hair, fair skin, cobalt eyes. Even though she was his sister, her beauty could not be denied. No wonder Dene had fallen in love with her. But she didn't belong to him, and he paid that price with his life—and his afterlife. After four thousand years, he had finally found the one. Zet felt it. Dene would be forced to help him win her hand—and speed was of the essence. Zet's body betrayed him. It had become harder to materialize—and soon he would be earth bound. Days, he only had days. He needed a plan, and he needed Dene and Tayla to make it come to fruition.

His insufferable curse would finally be over. And he would be free to live out his life as he chose. No more lessons from Dene.

No more once a century. His half-existence was a lie. The gods punished him more than they should. No matter if he had become flesh-and-bone from solstice to solstice, he needed to be free entirely. Those few months were not enough. The gods cursed him to suffer — to lie awake unable to move, unable to speak, unable to participate in life — but they bestowed kindness on Dene and his queen, they did not lie awake and suffer, they only became flesh at the appointed time. They did not have to suffer the curse as he did, especially his queen. She did not even know she was cursed.

Anubis, Isis, and Osiris had punished him with a living hell on earth — alert but frozen in a mummy's body, unable to move or speak for years at a time. The time had come for him to be free. And he would stop at nothing to get his life back. Even if it meant ruining another.

#

Bennett answered the phone on the fourth ring. He didn't want to appear anxious. His plan worked, and Tayla called.

"Bennett, I heard your house was broken into. Are you okay?"

"Tayla? Yes, thank God. I'm fine. But this just happened. How did you find out so quickly?"

"Don't worry about that. I just needed to know that you were all right. I'm happy nothing happened. I've got to go."

"Wait, before you go, would you like to go to lunch to discuss all this? I'm not sure I understand what's happening." There was a long silence on the other end of the phone. "Tayla, are you still there?" He could hear her breathing faster into the phone.

"I don't think that's a good idea."

"Why not? We can meet at Zia's. We loved going there."

"I can't. I have to go to my parents'."

"Is something wrong? Are they okay?" He knew exactly why she had to go to her parents'.

"They're fine. Their house was broken into as well. I am helping them with the police."

He had her talking to him again. He needed to keep it up. She told him about her parents. And he showed the right amount of concern. She had to see that he was the one for her.

"Okay, since lunch is off the table, let's do dinner. Nothing fancy. We need to talk."

"Let me think about it. I'll call you later. Goodbye, Bennett."

The phone went dead. His plan was working. She was going to call him. Tayla wanted a ring. She wanted to marry him. Bennett made up his mind. He would go to the jewelers and get her a ring, a big one. Something that would make her want to stay with him—that said, this was what she would have with him.

Before leaving, he took the key to Meredith's house and Tayla's car key. Meredith was next on his list. And taking Tayla's car was an added bonus. Bennett needed to keep her off balance, questioning everything. No way he would let up now. He had Tayla right where he wanted her.

#

Tayla finished checking out the storage room with Shalhoub and the detective. Nothing appeared to be missing, but there was sand on the floor. The detective pulled on gloves, took a bag from his pocket, and swept sand into it.

Tayla's mind swam with thoughts of the curse. She had sand at her house, sand in the exhibit hall, and sand in the storage room. Did her parents' house have sand? And did they find that same sand when they found Stan? What about Bennett's house? Could Zet be the one doing all of these things to make her believe in the curse? He didn't seem the type to do any work. But he was the type to want things his way. He could be trying to get to her.

What did she have that he could possibly want? According to Dene, he wanted to find his queen, the woman that could break the curse. And she was not his queen.

"Are we free to leave?" Shalhoub asked. "I've got to get back to the exhibit room."

"Yes. I'll be in touch with any further questions."

Shalhoub practically ran from the storage room. The detective turned to leave as well, but Tayla stopped him. "Detective, can you tell me what was on the notes left for Meredith and me? I need to know."

"The lab has them and is analyzing them."

He was avoiding the question. Tayla wanted to know. "I'm sure you read them. Please? I need to know."

The detective sighed, "I am watching you."

"This person is dangerous. What should we do? What about my parents? Bennett?"

"We're working on it. I've increased patrols in your neighborhood, and at Meredith's."

"What about my parents? And Bennett?"

"Ms. Amari, I assure you, we are doing all we can."

The detective's phone rang. He turned his back to Tayla. She strained to hear him, but he barely spoke, and when he did, she couldn't make it out.

"Something's come up. I've got to go but we're not finished here. I'll be in touch to finish this." He turned and shuffled down the hall.

Today sucked. First she couldn't sleep and came into work early. Then Dene showed up, and she felt the tension in the room. She couldn't even talk to him. Then she got a call from her parents about their house. And then when she was with the detective answering questions about her break-in and the museum break-in, she overheard that Bennett's house had been broken into.

To make matters worse, she found out what the note said. "I am watching you." Who was watching them? Her thoughts were all over the place. She couldn't think of anyone who would want to cause her harm. And she couldn't think of anyone who would want to hurt Meredith either. This had gone way beyond a practical joke.

Tayla knew that everything was related, she didn't know how, but she'd figure it out. Someone wanted them to be afraid. But who—and why? And how did Stan's death figure into all of this? It had to be related, but she just couldn't make the connection. She would, she wasn't giving up. Tayla just hoped that she'd figure it out before someone got hurt or something else happened.

Tayla took her time on the way back to the exhibit. She couldn't get Bennett out of her mind. Just talking to him for that short time hurt. When did things go so wrong? He seemed to be hurting, too. Should she meet him for dinner? Meredith would be all over her if she did. And if she met him, what would change? It would never work. To him, the job came first, and everything else second. She deserved better than second place.

She took a deep breath before going inside. So many things needed to be done. The exhibit fell further behind each time something else happened. The things that happened had her so scatterbrained. She couldn't concentrate on any one thing. Now, Bennett was a piece of the puzzle. A part of her still loved him. She guessed she would always hold a special place in her heart for him—they just couldn't be together.

Inside everyone was working on something. She glanced over at the wall Dene painted. The detail in the pictures astounded her. Beautiful. The best way she could sum it up. In another part of the room, Shalhoub worked on something at a table, and Meredith walked in from the behind the children's area carrying several boxes, followed by Zet pushing a cart full of artifacts.

Tayla heard Meredith's phone ringing. "I can grab that for you if you want."

Meredith replied, "Yes, thanks, Tay."

The voice on the other end — Detective Flanagan. "Detective, she's busy at the moment. Can I take a message?"

"I'll wait."

The room got cold. Something happened, she felt it. "Meredith, the detective needs to speak with you."

Meredith replied, "Take a message, please. I'm in the middle of something. I'll call him back."

"He said he'd wait. You'd better take this."

Meredith practically ran across the room.

"This is Meredith."

Silence filled the room. Meredith nodded every few seconds, and then slid to the floor before ending the call.

"I've got to go, Tay. My place — "

"Oh, no. Not you, too. First my parents, then Bennett, now you. I'll come with you."

"No. There's no use both of us leaving. Besides, we need to get this exhibit up before something else happens. I'll be fine."

Tayla hugged her and said, "It will be okay. Promise."

Meredith grabbed her things and ran out the door.

"She should not face this alone. I shall go with her," Zet said. He was out the door before anyone could say a word.

Tayla knew exactly how she felt. Tayla's stomach clenched, her heart beat faster. She could barely control her breathing. She yanked out the nearest chair and slumped into it, dropping her head into her hands. This day just kept getting worse. Sitting did nothing for her. She stood and paced. Sweat formed on her palms, and her head pounded in tandem with her racing heart.

Shalhoub's phone broke the silence. Moments later, he excused himself.

"I have a few things that I need to take care of. I will be back tomorrow. Dene can handle things here while I'm gone."

Shalhoub grabbed his briefcase and headed out the door, leaving Tayla alone with Dene. Everything was going to shit. She didn't want to be there alone with Dene—but that wasn't the case.

Dene walked gingerly over to Tayla. "We should talk. There is much to discuss."

Michele Jones

CHAPTER TWENTY-FIVE

Tayla got a reprieve when her phone rang. "Bennett. I told you I would call you... I can't make dinner... I'm just not ready for that...Goodbye."

Dene stood in front of Tayla, hands in his pockets. "Please, Tayla. We need to talk. I know you are angry with me, but I can fix this if you let me."

"Fix this? How are you going to fix this? Are you going to pull out a magic lamp, rub it, and have a genie appear?"

"I do not understand."

"Of course you don't. I think you use this language barrier to your advantage. I'm sure you know exactly what I'm saying. You just pretend to make me fall in love with you. And I did. I was such a fool."

"You are not a fool, and I did not want you to fall in love with me."

"Great. You just wanted to get me in bed. Well, it worked. I hope you're happy," Tayla yelled.

"Please. It is not like that."

"Really? Because it sure feels like that to me."

Dene paced, hands still shoved in his pockets. "There is so much you do not understand about me. I am not good for you. But I could not stay away from you. I wanted you."

"Right. You wanted me. Then you got me, and we know how that ended. You made up some bullshit story about being a four thousand-year-old cursed advisor to an evil pharaoh mummy, who is also cursed. Did I get that right?"

"It is not like that. I did not make up that story. And I still want you. You are all I think about. You consume my every thought, you are in my dreams. I see your smiling face, I smell your perfume. The gods are taunting me."

"You? They're taunting you? Give me a break. You flirt with me, you sleep with me, and then you lie to me. Then you try to blame it on the gods? I can't believe I'm listening to this."

"Please give me a chance. I really am telling the truth."

"Get away from me!" she screamed at him.

Dene turned to leave, but stopped. "What if I could prove it?"

"Prove what? That I'm an idiot for falling for you? For thinking we had a chance?" Tayla paced across the floor. "How could I be so stupid?"

Dene crossed the room and spun Tayla toward him. He looked her in the eyes, and wrapped his arms around her, crushing his lips to hers. She pulled back at first, but slowly relaxed, returning the kiss.

He broke the kiss, both of them breathing hard. "Tayla, I want you to know, I love you. I tried to fight it, but I cannot fight it any longer. Please, give me a second chance."

Her voice cracked as she spoke. "You love me?"

He closed his eyes. "I pray the gods forgive me. I want you. Now. Forever. I will take whatever you give me. A day, two days, a week. Please. Say you love me."

Tayla ran her fingers across her lips—they tingled from his kiss. "I—" She couldn't control herself. She pulled him to her and inhaled deeply. One hand reached up, and she ran her fingers through his hair. Her other hand slid down his chest while she traced his lips with her tongue.

He sucked in a deep breath but didn't pull away from her. She knew she had him. And she wasn't letting go.

#

Dene propped himself up on his elbows and watched Tayla go around the room gathering her clothes. A smile crossed his face knowing he held her lace thong. How long would he let her search?

Tayla sauntered over to Dene and straddled him, then she leaned down close to his face. "Do you have my thong?" Tayla whispered into his ear then nibbled on his earlobe.

He wrapped one arm around her and pulled her to his chest. The other hand caressed her round breast while he kissed her lightly on the lips. The way her body responded got him excited him again. He pulled her thong out and twirled it in front of her. She reached for it, but he pulled it back.

She breathed harder. He loved the way she felt on top of him.

"What will you give me for it?"

"Let me get dressed. Then take me home, and you'll find out."

The thought of going home with Tayla sent chills down his spine. He lifted her off him and stood, pulling her up to her feet. He dangled her panties again, this time handing them to her when she reached for them. Tayla bent over, stepped into them, and started pulling them up. He leaned in and kissed her, grabbed her hands and helped her pull her panties on—slowly. He drew his rough hands up her thighs while he nibbled on her neck and rested his hands on her hips.

"Not here." Her voice was husky, breathless. "Please. Let's go do this at my place."

Dene backed away, letting go of her hands. "I would like that very much." He hurried into his boxers, jeans, and polo, never taking his eyes off her. Goosebumps spread up his arms as she pulled on her silky cami. Sweat beaded on his upper lip as she pulled on her jeans.

Things changed. He knew his time was limited, but he no longer wanted to deny himself the pleasure he found. He may never have the chance again. "Before we go to your house, let us stop for something to eat. I am starving."

"What are you hungry for?"

"Besides you?" He smiled when she blushed. "I would like pizza."

"Zia's makes great pizza, and it's on the way to my house."

Her phone rang, ruining the moment. "We can't do lunch. The detective wants me to come to the station, now. But I'm free for dinner."

Dene's stomach growled. He frowned. "I would love to eat dinner with you. I shall escort you to the police station, and I will wait for you there. When you finish, we can go to your pizza place."

"Thanks. But I don't know how long I'll be. Let me call you, and we can meet at Zia's when I'm done."

"I do not mind waiting for you."

"It's not fair to you. You said you have things you need to do. Please, go home. When I'm done, I'll text you the address."

He did not want to leave her, but he agreed.

#

Bennett couldn't believe that Tayla wouldn't have dinner with him. He thought he had her where he wanted her. What else did he need to do to make her realize she belonged to him?

And if she didn't come to her senses and come back to him, he would make sure she wouldn't be with anyone else, either.

He even had the police fooled—made them think it was someone using the mummy's curse. Even a threatening note—I am watching you. And he was careful. He didn't use his car or his phone. He even used clothes that were different than anything he normally wore.

Surely Tayla needed him to comfort her. He reached into his pocket and pulled out his cell. Five rings and no answer—voicemail—he hung up and shoved the phone back in his pocket. He wouldn't give up. He had other plans. Was she with some other guy? Is that why she didn't answer his call? Tayla had better not be if she knew what was good for her—and the other guy.

That independent streak in her would be her demise. Bennett went to his locker and took out the keys he made copies of from Tayla's and shoved them into his front pocket. He ran his hand through his hair and paced the locker room. Since she didn't respond to any of the things he had done thus far, he needed to take it to the next level.

Before he went to the police station as the detective directed him to, he would take care of Tayla's car. He wouldn't do anything that would harm her, but he would have some fun at her expense — moving her car so she couldn't find it.

Bennett took his phone out and called Tayla again. This time she answered. "Hey."

"Uh, um, Bennett. Hi."

"I'm so glad I got you. You okay?"

"I'm fine. What did you want?"

She sounded so — sad. "Just checking to see how you were.

"I'm doing okay."

"Let's get together, soon. We really need to talk. "

"Goodbye, Bennett."

She missed him. He knew she still loved him. He could tell by her reaction to his call. He shoved his hands into his pockets, playing with the ring box in one and the keys in the other. Time to put his next steps into action. But he might as well have some fun while he waited for Tayla to come to her senses.

Bennett texted Dr. Coldwell. Since he wasn't doing dinner with Tayla, he would go to Zia's with Debra. And later, well, Debra's place would be just fine.

CHAPTER TWENTY-SIX

Dene materialized at the house they shared after he dropped Tayla off at the police station. He saw Shalhoub in the kitchen and Zet lounging on the couch. Things between Shalhoub and Zet had not improved.

"Where have you been? Shalhoub has been here for hours."

Dene gritted his teeth. "I had a few things to take care of."

"Such as?" Zet asked. "I should be your number one priority."

"You have always been. But no more. You do not care. You learn nothing. You are no better than you were four thousand years ago."

"Enough. You know that I am trying."

Dene laughed. "You are not. You are still self-centered, you care for no one, you are rude—"

"Don't forget, he killed that security guard," Shalhoub said.

Killing that security guard sealed their fate this century. They would not pass into the afterlife. "You will not pass the weighing of the heart test. You have cost me my chance at happiness once again."

"I cost you nothing. It is your fault. You have not taught me well enough."

"The gods cursed us both. I have lived up to my end of the bargain. And I have tried to redeem you. You are unredeemable. You will not pass the test."

"I have a plan."

Dene knew what Zet's plan was. It would not work, Meredith had no interest in him. Zet's plans never worked. Was that part of the curse? If only he would reform. Become a better person. Stop hurting others. Perhaps then he would pass the weighing ceremony.

How many chances would the gods afford them? For centuries he had been trying with no luck. Would the gods take pity on him and let him move on without Zet? Or would he be forced to spend his eternity living out this curse?

How long before Tayla texted? He could not wait to get out of there.

Dene stalked off to his room. He did not want to be around Zet, and Shalhoub did nothing to make things easier. He flopped down on the bed. He did not want to be there either. He would take a shower. He loved the way the scalding hot water fell from the metal shower head, pulsing on his body.

Fifteen minutes later, the water turned colder. He got out and wrapped a towel around his waist. As he started down the hall, he heard his phone ringing. It had to be Tayla. He ran to answer it but missed it. He looked at the screen — missed call. Tayla. He hit redial. She had finished at the police station and couldn't wait to meet him for dinner.

He selected the jeans that Meredith convinced him to buy, a forest green oxford shirt, and a brown leather jacket. Cologne and Dockside's finished his outfit.

Dene walked down the hall, past Shalhoub and Zet who sat on opposite sides of the couch.

"Going somewhere?" Zet asked.

"I'm meeting someone for dinner."

"Get it while you can. Since you are not helping me pass my lessons."

He stopped and his body tensed. "It is time you help yourself. Perhaps if you would be more humble, you could pass one test. Now if you will excuse me, I am leaving."

Shalhoub asked, "Where are you going to dinner?"

"A pizza place called Zia's. I have been told they make the best pizza."

#

Tayla got there before Dene. The owner recognized her and greeted her warmly. "Tayla. How are you?"

"Giuseppe, I'm fine. How are you?"

"I'm good. Follow me. Your table has not been taken yet. Where is Bennett?"

"I'm actually meeting someone else tonight. Would you mind if we sat in the other room? Away from the noise?"

"*Va bene.*"

"What?"

"Okay, follow me." Giuseppe led her away to a table in the other room, close to the bar. Tayla pointed to a table in the back where she couldn't be easily seen.

"What can I get you to drink?"

"Guinness, and would you mind starting an order of bruschetta?"

"I'll get them started. Donna will be your server."

Zia's was getting busy. People kept coming in. But not Dene. Maybe he wasn't coming. Of course he was coming. She was being silly. How long before he got there? She looked at her watch. Back at the people coming in. He should be there by now. Drummed her fingers on the table. Looked at her watch again. Back to the bar.

Nerves were getting to her. She didn't want him to see her anxious. Would it work out between them? Her legs bounced a thousand miles a minute. Tayla took a deep breath to calm down. She was having trouble with the thought of him being a four-thousand-year-old cursed mummy. But the sand that the detective found? How could she ignore that?

She pulled out her phone to text him, but decided against it. She didn't want to appear anxious. Moments later, she saw Dene walk in.

The wait for him to get to her table had her stomach in knots. How long did it to walk across the room? Only seconds had passed but it felt like hours. Finally, he arrived at their table. They greeted each other before he sat. The server asked for his drink order and left after getting it. Alone. With Dene. No one else around her held her interest. Her senses went into overdrive when she breathed in his earthy cinnamon scent. It intoxicated her. She remembered the scent, but she knew no one else wore it. Strange. So much she needed to understand.

Dene reached across the table, took her hand, and smiled at her. Breathe, Tayla. Her heartbeat sped up. Calm down. She heard his stomach growl. "You better look at the menu. I don't want you saying that I starved you."

"You told me that you come here often. Please order what you wish. If you love it, I am sure that I will."

Donna set his drink in front of him and her bruschetta. "What can I get ya?"

"We'd like a large hand tossed. Light sauce, pepperoni, green olive, sausage, and hot pepper."

The server smiled. Giuseppe thought you would order that. It'll be out shortly. Anything else for ya?"

"What if I didn't order that? What would you do with the pizza?"

"According to Giuseppe, you order the same thing every time you come. The only thing different is the appetizer or salads. If you ordered something different, the staff would eat it."

After Donna left, Tayla started the conversation. "I am trying, but it's difficult for me to wrap my head around what you said. The practical side of me wants proof. My heart says let it go."

Tayla sucked in a deep breath before Dene could answer. Her face grew hot and her hands shook. She dropped her head but stared at the couple walking arm-in-arm and laughing as they followed Donna toward the back of the restaurant.

"What is wrong?"

"It's—it's nothing. Sorry. Back to us, please."

"I need you to believe in me, to trust me," Dene said. "This is an extremely complicated situation."

"Okay, we'll come back to this later. Can you at least tell me why Zet believes that Meredith is the reincarnated queen? Or is that some secret that you can't share, either?"

Dene pulled his hand back, folded his arms across his chest, and took a deep breath. "Meredith looks like our queen—Zet's wife and sister. She also has the same tattoo on her shoulder as did our queen, the symbol of the goddess Neith, two arrows crossed over a shield.

"Oh my God." Tayla felt sweat running down the back of her neck. "So the tattoo and her looks are the reason Zet believes she is the reincarnated queen? No other reason?"

"He needs no other reason. To him, that is all that matters. But the queen, she—"

Donna came delivered their pizza and served them each a slice. "Can I get you anything else? Another beer?"

"None for me, just a large water please," Tayla replied.

"Water for me as well, thank you."

They ate in silence while they waited for their drinks. After Donna dropped them off the conversation continued.

"What were you going to say about the queen before you were interrupted?"

"Our queen, she was soft spoken. Modest. I am not sure that is the correct word. But the tattoo is the main reason he believes she is the queen. Happily, Meredith does not care for him. I would not want to see her get hurt by Zet."

"So the tattoo. That is his deciding factor?"

"He has said so. I believe there is more than looks and a tattoo. Meredith is a wonderful person, but her personality is all wrong. You behave most like our queen. The way you treat others, your kindness. You even wear a similar cologne scent that she wore. You treat others as did our queen. You listen to them. Hear what they have to say. You conduct yourself in a regal fashion."

"Dene—"

"Please do not take what I said as a slight against your friend. She is a nice person as well. She made me feel welcome. She—"

Tayla raised her voice. "Dene."

He looked at her. "What?"

"Meredith is not the only person that has that tattoo."

"I do not understand."

"The tattoo of Neith, we both have it. I loved the stela when I saw it. We both wanted to get ink, something meaningful to us. So we each got a Neith's stela tattoo. Meredith on her shoulder, mine on my thigh. My parents didn't want me to get one, so I chose a spot where my parents couldn't see it. Didn't you see it?"

"I saw a tattoo on your thigh. But that was not what I focused on. I preferred to look at your beautiful face."

Tayla felt her face heat up.

#

Dene stared at Tayla. How could he have missed that? Most importantly, could she be the queen? Is that what the gods had tried to tell him? Everything came together. Cologne. Manners. Acts of kindness. Even the way they made love. Meredith was not the reincarnated queen. Tayla was.

Zet had it all wrong. Looks and a tattoo were not what made the queen. How could he have been so stupid? For thousands of years they looked for someone that *resembled* the queen. Instead they should have been looking for someone that *acted* like their queen.

He succeeded. He was the lucky one. The queen had been found, and if he were lucky enough, she would be the one that lifted this insufferable curse. He would be free at last, and living with his true love. Now he needed to convince her to choose him. And time ran short. Should he show her? The only proof he could provide would be dematerializing. But his powers were failing, and soon he would not be able to do so. And even if he did, would that be enough to keep her from breaking the curse? So much to consider.

And what if she did not truly love him? All signs indicated that she did, but what if he were wrong? Could he live with that kind of rejection? Losing her once was difficult. Losing her a second time would devastate him. That would be something he could not possibly recover from.

No, he would not chance losing her. He would show her how much he loved her. How much they were meant to be together. If he read the signs correctly, she loved him, too. She had said so.

All those cryptic messages from the gods. In their way, they tried to lead him to her. Dene had to believe that. Everything had fallen into place. Best of all, Tayla had broken up with her boyfriend and was free to be with him. He would not be responsible for their ruined relationship.

Dene looked up from his plate and into Tayla's eyes. She looked—stunned. Maybe that was not the correct word. Everything she thought she knew had changed. Things that could not possibly be true had come to light. And he was part of that.

He managed to eat a few slices of pizza while he pondered their fate. He offered a quick prayer to the gods to help him through this, then he reached for her hand.

Tayla kept looking to the back of the restaurant. What could be there that captured her attention?

"What is wrong? Do we need to leave?"

Tayla nibbled on her slice. "Northing's wrong. Thought I saw someone I knew. Turns out I was wrong. Let's finish and go back to my place for dessert."

"I would love that."

#

Bennett saw Tayla with another man. Holding hands. Laughing. Eating at their favorite restaurant. How dare she? That bitch. Who did she think she was? She belonged to him. No way would he let this happen. She gave him no choice. If he couldn't have her, no one would.

"Debra, would you excuse me? I'll be right back. I see an old friend of my father's."

"Certainly. But hurry back. Dinner should be here any time."

He threw his napkin on the table, walked over to her, gave her a peck on the cheek, and then strode to Tayla's table.

"Tayla."

"Bennett."

"I thought you said you weren't ready to go out. Yet here you are."

"I said I wasn't ready to go out with you. You remember my colleague, Dene?"

Colleague. Right. She isn't fooling me. He must be the owner of the glass of wine he saw at her house the other day. He'd take care of him too. "Good evening, Dene." His tone cool.

Dene extend his hand. "Nice to see you again, Bennett."

Bennett ignored his hand and faced only Tayla. In a voice barely above a whisper he addressed her. "You said give you time. I didn't think that meant you'd be out with other men."

Tayla stared directly into his eyes. "This isn't the place. Goodbye, Bennett."

"This isn't over by a long shot." He spun around and left.

Michele Jones

CHAPTER TWENTY-SEVEN

Tayla asked their server for a box. She needed to get out of there. Never did it occur to her that she would see Bennett there. And with another woman. Yet he had the nerve to confront her about her date. She let out a groan.

Their server brought over a box and the bill. Dene reached into his pocket, pulled out his wallet and threw enough down to cover the bill and tip.

"I invited you for dinner. I'll pay." She shoved his money toward him.

He lay his hand over top of hers. "I would like to pay. Let us take our pizza and leave."

Dene rose and walked to Tayla's side of the table. "Allow me." He pulled her chair back and helped her up.

Tayla could feel her face heat up. As Dene wrapped his arm around her waist, goosebumps formed on her arms. Did he notice that? Her heart beat pounded her chest like a jackhammer. She could barely breathe. The promise of an evening with Dene made her shutter.

With his free hand, Dene removed his jacket and wrapped it around her shoulders. "How is that?"

She wasn't cold. His touch lit her skin on fire. She leaned into his shoulder and inhaled deeply, taking in his smell. It aroused her. She didn't want the walk to her car to end, but her car was only a block away. When they arrived, she pulled back and unlocked the door with her fob. Always the gentleman, Dene opened the door for her, holding her hand as she entered. "Do you want me to drop you off at your car? Or would you like to ride with me?"

Tayla got her answer when he walked around the other side of the car and slid inside. His cologne permeated the car when she turned the heat on, and his easy attitude made the trip a pleasure. Her lips tingled in anticipation of another romantic evening, and her body responded well. "I don't have anything for dessert. Let's stop at the store and get something."

"You do not need to feed me dessert. I will be okay just spending time with you."

Her face felt flush. She must be on fire. "I need a couple of things. Do you mind?"

"I do not. But let us make it fast. I wish to spend my evening with you in comfort, not at a store."

The store parking lot was empty—she got a place in front. Dene was fast. He was out of the car and opening her door before she had her keys out of the ignition. Tayla leaned in to get her purse, and Dene rested his hand on her back. It sent shivers up her spine, and she pulled his jacket tighter around her shoulders.

Tayla was fast. She got what she needed, some chocolate, and something in the woman's isle. Dene grabbed the bags from the self-checkout and once again slid his hand around her waist.

"Would you like me to drive?"

She said nothing, but dropped the key in his outstretched hand. He selected a jazz music station and took his time driving them to her house.

"You'll have to park down the street. There's never any parking near my house."

"Then it is a good thing that I escorted you home. A beautiful woman such as you should not be alone, especially since your home has been broken into."

Dene grabbed the pizza and the bags from the back of the car. They had to park two blocks away.

"It's such a nice night. I'm glad you were here to share it with me. Thanks for coming home with me." She stood on her toes and kissed him lightly on the lips. He dropped what he was carrying and pulled her closer to him. Her breath caught in her throat. "Don't stop."

"We should not do this out here. Let us continue to your house." He bent over and picked up the pizza and the grocery bag.

Tayla sighed. "You're right. She took his hand and started walking to her house. As they got closer to her house, Tayla's hair stood on end. A queasy feeling settled in the pit of her stomach.

"Is something wrong? Why did you stop?"

"I—I don't know. I have a bad feeling."

#

Bennett paced on the side of her house. How did he get to her house before she did? Did she stop somewhere with that guy?

This couldn't be happening. How could she do this to him? She belonged to him. How could she dump him for that, that idiot? A coworker. Not even a doctor. What did she see in him, anyway?

The pacing continued. Eyes peeled for any sign of her. Finally, he saw her car. She'd be here soon. Bennett pulled out his key and let himself inside. No use airing dirty laundry outside.

He planned to settle this mess now. Make her see the error of her ways. It would take a minute or two for her to get here, the street was parked solid — as usual. Bennett poured himself a glass of wine from the fridge, poured another glass for her. He sat on the couch and waited. Stared at the door. Where the hell was she? It didn't take that long to walk down the street.

Footsteps, then keys jingled. It was time for her to come back to him. The door opened, and both Tayla and Dene stepped inside, breathing heavy and holding hands.

Bennett bolted off the couch and threw his glass of wine to the floor. "It took you long enough to get here. I've been waiting for you."

"How? What? Get out."

"Is that any way to treat your boyfriend?"

"We're not together any more. And we will never be together again. Get out!"

Bennett laughed as Dene positioned himself between him and Tayla. Did he really think he could protect her?"

"You belong to me. I've waited long enough for you to come to your senses." He pulled out a gun and aimed it at both of them.

#

Tayla shook. "Bennett, you don't want this. Please, just go home."

"I'm not leaving. Either you agree to come back to me and leave lover boy, or I'll be forced to take action."

Sirens blared in the background. Did the detective know she was in trouble? He told her they were watching the house, extra patrols. Maybe they saw Bennett come inside. "You don't mean that."

"Of course I mean it. Nobody breaks up with me." He paced and ran his free hand through his hair.

"Let's talk about this tomorrow, when you've had a chance to think about it. Cool off."

"Don't tell me to what I should do. This could have all been avoided if you would have come back to me after I broke into your house. But no. You didn't even call me."

"That was you?"

"Of course it was me. Did you really think you were so important that anyone would want to harm you? You're nobody."

Tayla pushed past Dene, crossed the room, and stood in front of Bennett. "If I'm such a nobody, then why do you even want me?"

"I told you. Nobody breaks up with me."

"How could you?"

"Please. You're nothing. I made you what you are. Now tell your little friend to go away, and I'll forget everything you did and take you back."

"I'm not going back with you. I can't believe I ever loved you. How could you be so cruel?"

The sirens stopped. Or she imagined them. They were alone. With a madman. Things just got worse.

\#

Dene just found the love he had been searching for for four thousand years. He couldn't lose her. He heard the footsteps on the porch, he watched Bennett lose control. He saw him pull the trigger on the gun. No time to think, he had to react. Tayla did not move. The bullet headed straight for her. Dene pushed her out of the way, and the bullet struck him in the chest.

The pain seared through his chest. He fell to the floor.

Dene struggled to breathe. He lay helpless as Tayla crawled toward him. Tears ran down her cheeks.

"Oh my God, Bennett. What have you done?"

Bennett stood there, staring. Seconds later, Detective Flanagan burst through the door, followed by several officers with guns drawn.

"Please. Help him. Call an ambulance. Bennett shot him." Tayla pulled the afghan from the couch, knelt next to Dene, and covered his chest. She pressed the cloth tight on it. "You're going to be all right. I'm here. Stay with me."

Bennett spun and pointed the gun at the police.

Detective Flanagan shouted, "Drop the gun."

Bennett didn't move, nor did he drop the gun. Dene coughed and held Tayla's hand on his chest. The pained look in her eyes spoke volumes.

Things appeared to be happening in slow motion. Bennett swung the gun back and forth between the detective and the officers.

Once again the detective yelled, "Drop the gun."

Instead of listening, Bennett pulled the trigger. The detective fired back, shooting Bennett in the chest.

"Oh my God!" Tayla screamed.

Bennett crumpled to the floor.

She didn't move from Dene. "Please, don't die. I believe you." She bent her head over and sobbed uncontrollably.

Dene's gasped for air, and tried to speak. Only garbled sounds came out.

"Please, don't try to talk."

Dene smiled at Tayla, and then the room went black.

#

Zet turned to the gods. "What am I doing here?"

To his left he saw Dene and someone else.

Anubis spoke in a deep thunderous voice. "Silence. We have summoned you here to discuss your fate. The curse has been broken. Dene has found the queen."

Dene turned toward the gods. "Praise the gods. But why now? I find my true love, and I shall die before we can be together."

Isis walked over and addressed him. "Dene, be silent. We will speak with you later."

Zet laughed as he observed Bennett. His confusion, seeing the green-skinned half-mummy, half-Pharaoh-like man, Osiris.

Bennett asked. "What's going on? Who the hell are you? What the hell am I doing here? "

Osiris towered over Bennett. "Speak not. Your fate has yet to be determined."

Zet wanted to be done with this. Clearly Dene had been mortally wounded. He may have won the queen's heart, but he would not be around to enjoy it. The curse had been broken. He would be free to live his life out as a human.

The gods showed all the world below. Men in uniforms with a bed on wheels working on both Dene and Bennett. Tayla standing to the side of Dene, crying.

"It is time to discuss your part of the curse," Anubis said.

"I can hardly wait. Finally, I shall be free. You have punished me long enough."

"Silence." Anubis' voice boomed over everyone. "Djzet, the curse has been lifted. The queen has chosen another. The curse is clear. Your soul shall be released to atone as a mortal. You will no longer be immortal and revived each century to learn your lessons as written in the Book of the Dead, but rather you shall live as a mortal, with only your memories of the past to guide you."

Free. Finally free. No more lessons. No more searching. And best of all, he still would be free to choose whomever he wanted to be with. Though, he may pursue the former queen. She was beautiful. And Dene did want her.

Osiris, the god of the afterlife turned to Zet. "Do you accept the terms as we have explained them to you?"

Dene spoke. "Osiris, I am ready to cross to the afterlife."

Isis lifted her hand. "We are not ready to speak with you yet, Dene."

The gods turned to Bennett. Zet watched, waiting to see why the human had joined them. "He is not of our world. Why have you brought him here?"

"Silence, Djzet." All the gods responded at once.

Anubis turned to Bennett. "Your soul is not pure, and your wound is mortal. You have been brought here to atone for hurting the queen. As punishment, your soul shall be cast into the underworld."

Bennett opened his mouth, but nothing came out. A black mist filled the room. It surrounded Bennett, closing in. Bennett spun around, looking for a way out. He screamed, but the mist closed in tighter. "Please. No. Help me," he pleaded. "I don't deserve this."

All watched as the mist enveloped Bennett. He flailed his arms, trying to push the mist away.

"No. Please. I'll change. You don't understand. Tayla's my girlfriend."

It was useless. The black mist tightened around him and sucked his soul out of his body. The soulless vessel slumped to the floor.

The gods turned to Zet. Anubis spoke. "The curse allows you to live your life as a mortal, to atone for your sins. And this you shall do." Anubis, Isis, and Osiris surrounded him, each laying a hand on him. Djzet struggled, but could not move. Anubis pulled his soul from his body, and suspended it in the air. "Behold, your new vessel." Moments later, Djzet's soul had been placed into Bennett's lifeless body.

"But this isn't what you promised. I am to be free to live out my life."

"It is what you deserve."

"And Dene, now for you and your destiny."

Michele Jones

CHAPTER TWENTY-EIGHT

Tayla didn't want to leave Dene's side. "Please, let me ride with him." The paramedics refused.

The detective walked over to her and put his arm around her. "I'll take you to the hospital. I'd like to get your statement. You can talk as we drive. Officer Gray will drive."

Before they left, she called Meredith to fill her in.

The ten-minute ride to the hospital seemed to take forever. The detective asked his questions, and she answered. He took notes, but used his phone to record the conversation. There wasn't much to say. Bennett lost it. He tried to kill her, Dene stepped in front of her and took the bullet, saving her life. The police arrived, Bennett got shot. Everything was a blur. She shook her head in disbelief. Why?

Meredith ran to her as she walked into the waiting room. The questions flew. "Are you okay? What about Dene? What happened?"

"Mer, I'm glad you're here. Thanks for coming."

"Of course I'm here for you. I just can't believe it. I never thought he would do something like this."

Tayla sighed. "I don't know what happened. It went so wrong so fast."

The detective put up his hand. "Ms. Nazari, would you mind if I asked you a few questions?"

They went to the back of the room and talked for quite some time. Meredith sat close to him, and when they finally finished, Meredith came back to Tayla.

"He told me everything. Thank God for the extra patrols and the neighborhood watch. Now, let's get a coffee and talk. They'll be in surgery for a while."

They went to the coffee pot, it was off. The only choice, vending machine coffee. At least she could get some M&Ms. Her nerves were shot. They fed the machine and got coffee for themselves and the detective. Tayla got her M&Ms, and Meredith got some chips. They returned to the seating area, and handed the detective his coffee. He left them to talk for a moment, then returned. He seemed to have endless questions.

Several hours later and several more questions, the waiting room patient information phone rang. After hours, anyone waiting was instructed to answer. Tayla jumped up and answered it.

"They're in recovery. The doctor said we can see them after they wake and get into their own rooms. Someone will call down and let us know."

The detective jumped up and addressed both of them. "I have officers stationed outside of Bennett's door. I will let them know to let you in, Tayla."

"Thank you. I will make it brief."

Another couple hours passed before the phone rang. Meredith jerked her head off the detective's shoulder, and Tayla jumped out of the chair. They weren't the only ones waiting, but she hoped the call was for them. A nervous man answered the phone. He rubbed his hand over his face.

"Family of Bennett Hawthorne."

Tayla rose and gingerly walked to the phone. She nodded a few times and hung up. She sulked back and flopped down in her chair. "Bennett has been moved to his room."

"Are you going up?" Meredith asked.

"Not until I hear something about Dene."

The words no sooner came out of her mouth when the phone rang again. Once again the anxious-looking man grabbed the phone.

"Family of Dene Tahan."

Tayla ran to the phone. She came back and relayed that Dene had been moved to his room. "I'm going up."

#

Tayla took the elevator to the fourth floor. Intensive care. The smell of antiseptic made her gag. The beeping of the monitors made her nervous. People die there. If that happened to Dene, even Bennett, she couldn't take that. The nurses' station to her left was deserted. The sounds of a rolling cart, moaning patients, and muffled conversations came from down the hall.

What room had they been called to? Would they make it? Was it someone she knew? Bennett? Dene? She said a silent prayer.

A nurse came down the hall and addressed her. "What are you doing here? Visiting hours don't start until 9:30. You'll have to come back."

"I received a call telling me that Bennett Hawthorn and Dene Tahan were taken here. They said I could visit for a few minutes."

The nurse sighed. "Sorry. Busy night. Who do you want to see first?"

"Bennett Hawthorn."

The nurse took her up the hall and around to the right. The walked down that hall, and made another right, and followed that hall to the end and made another right. The nurse took her the long way. Why?

She got her answer. A cart was being wheeled from a room a few feet down the hall, covered by a sheet, being escorted by a sobbing male. Her stomach lurched. Bile rose into her mouth. Tayla offered another prayer for someone she didn't know. She breathed harder. Please, God. Let them make it.

The officers stationed outside Bennett's room looked up, but didn't move to let her in. "Detective Flanagan should have called. I'm Tayla Amari. He said I could go in and see him for just one moment."

One of the officers pulled out a phone and made a call. "The detective confirmed it. You can go inside."

Tayla pushed open the door and went in.

Bennett lay still on the bed. IVs in his arms. She crept to the bed and leaned on the rails. "Bennett. Why?"

She wanted closure. She leaned in closer and saw his hands cuffed to the bed. Her body shook. "What happened to you, Bennett? You took a shot at me. I would probably be dead if Dene hadn't saved me. In time, we could have been friends. Now, you deserve whatever happens to you."

She paced the room. The sterile smell nauseated her. She stood by his side again. "And Stan the guard? And Meredith's brother? All in the name of a curse? Just to get back at me? Why? This isn't like you. You've changed. Everything's changed. Instead of healing people, you are going to jail. You're going to be alone. After your trial, you'll never see me again. I want nothing to do with you ever again."

She saw his eyes flutter. He looked like he tried to reach for her.

"I am not Bennett. I am Djzet. Egyptian Pharaoh."

"Bennett? You've lost it. Rest. Someone will check on you. When I walk out that door, you'll never have to worry about me again."

With those words she left. Outside his room, she shook and a tear ran down her cheek. She sniffed, wiped the tear, and headed back to the nurses' station. She had to see Dene.

The nurse gave her his room number. No escort this time. The halls had quieted.

Tayla tiptoed to his room. She calmed herself by taking a deep breath before going inside. More tubes, IVs, beeping monitors, and antiseptic smell. "Please, God. Let him be okay."

As she neared his bed she saw his eyelids flutter. Could he be awake? She grabbed his hand, leaned in, and kissed him tenderly on his lips. "Please, don't try and talk. The doctor said you needed your rest. That you should recover. That you needed to take it easy."

She dropped his hand and paced near his bed. "You saved me," she whispered. "I owe you my life. But if you die, my life will be empty. I know now that we were meant to be together. I denied it for so long. The connection that I felt to you. How you made me feel. How we belong together."

"Tayla."

"I'm right here. Please, the doctors said you shouldn't speak."

"I said I would show you. That I could prove it. But now... I can no longer... I'm mortal now."

"Ssh. It's okay. I believe you. Please just rest."

The room filled with a mist and three figures took shape. She recognized them immediately — Anubis, Isis, and Osiris.

"Queen MerNeith, this is your opportunity for a second chance. The curse has been broken."

Seconds later the room was empty, and her memory restored. She remembered everything. She was Queen MerNeith, and he was her beloved.

Dene's eyelids fluttered again. His hand moved ever so slightly. Tayla took his hand again into hers. "I love you. I've always loved you. This, finally, is our second chance."

Dear Reader,

Thank you for taking the time to read Romance Under Wraps. If you enjoyed it, please consider telling your friends and posting a short review. Word of mouth is an author's best friend, helps more than you could possibly know, and is much appreciated.

~Michele

About the Author

Michele Jones has always been a fan of the fictional world. Whether thriller, suspense, paranormal, or fantasy, she enjoys getting lost in the written word.

She started writing stories with her best friend when she was younger. She has written for her high school newspaper and local community newsletters. Now Michele writes for herself producing short stories, memoirs, and novels in many genres.

Michele is proud to be one of three authors in her family, and hopes to one day do a collaboration with her sister and her daughter.

She loves spending time with her family and friends, inspiring young writers and cooking. To learn more about her, visit http://michele-jones.com.

www.ingramcontent.com/pod-product-compliance
Lightning Source LLC
Chambersburg PA
CBHW071304250626
47159CB00004B/1301